PRINCESS TIARA AND THE CROWN OF VIRTUES

A TEENAGE FAIRY TALE ADVENTURE

JANET FICHTER

AT JESUS FEET PUBLISHING

Princess Tiara and the Crown of Virtues: A Teenage Fairy Tale Adventure

Published by At Jesus Feet Publishing
Lakewood, CO 80215

ISBN: 979-8-9869132-0-9
Library of Congress Control Number (LCCN): 2022919592
CIP Data Block Available upon request
YOUNG ADULT FICTION / Fairy Tales & Folklore / General

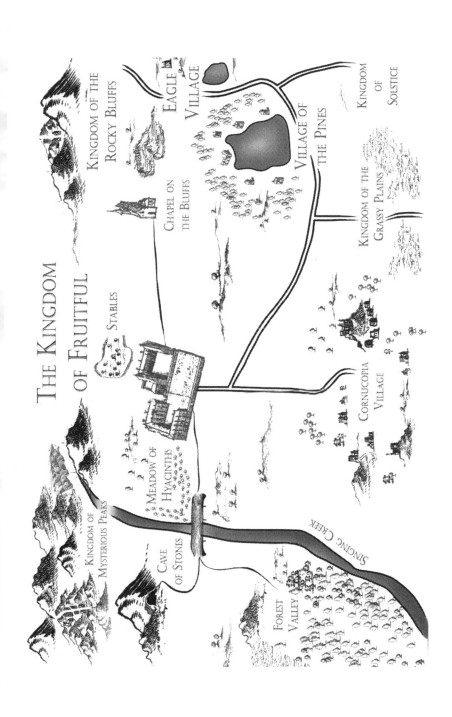

The Kingdom of Fruitful

KINGDOM OF MYSTERIOUS PEAKS

CAVE OF STONES

MEADOW OF HYACINTHS

STABLES

KINGDOM OF THE ROCKY BLUFFS

CHAPEL ON THE BLUFFS

EAGLE VILLAGE

VILLAGE OF THE PINES

KINGDOM OF SOLSTICE

KINGDOM OF THE GRASSY PLAINS

CORNUCOPIA VILLAGE

FOREST VALLEY

SINGING CREEK

Contents

Dedication

To my amazing nieces and nephews. You have each blessed the world in the most remarkable ways. Writing this story to honor and celebrate your unique and wonderful virtues is the only way I know to tell you how dearly I love you. You inspire me always.

To my wonderful husband who has once again come alongside me in this endeavor. Your strength, patience, and perspective guide me in ways you will never know. You are my steady, and I love you to the depths.

To the many students I've instructed over the years and all who will read this story. May you choose to walk in virtue, and may you be surrounded by others who do the same. The world needs you.

To the Author of Life. With praise and thanksgiving, I offer this story to Your glory.

Introduction

(Two Years Hence)

Atop the grassy knoll, Princess Tiara held tightly to the reins of the white Arabian. She forced her trembling knees to lock, for on the mighty stallion sat the warrior crusader who had delivered her kingdom. *Breathe, Tiara, breathe.* She steadied herself. *The kingdom is safe now.*

With her free hand, she caressed the special gift of the soft, multi-colored cloak in which she had hidden her crown in case of capture. "Thank you, Old One," she whispered as a tribute to the guardian who had watched over her family for years. She freed the crown from its protective covering and held it firmly.

Realizing the crusader overheard her spoken thoughts, she centered herself with another deep breath. His powerful presence brought conflicting emotions. As if in unison with Tiara's exhale, the massive steed snorted, his restive pawing indicating it was time to ride.

With her sight fixed on the horizon, the princess resisted the urge to turn back and look up. *He's watching. I must be brave.* She yearned to study the warrior's fierce, reassuring eyes one last time. His resolve would provide the strength she needed to head home.

Tiara forced herself to let go of the reins. She took a courageous step forward as the wind danced with her long brown hair. Though the bronze breastplate sheltered her from the gust's strength, a swirling breeze carried her gaze down the knoll to the Kingdom of Fruitful, the beloved empire they'd fought to save. The afternoon air echoed her thoughts. *My time as a soldier is over. I am a princess once again, and I must return to the castle.*

Tiara studied the sparkling gems in her crown, her fingers tracing each one. Then, with a nod of confidence, she placed the crown atop her head for the first time in weeks. With a swift glance back, she found needed assurance in the eyes of the kingdom's redeemer. Emboldened, Princess Tiara lifted her head high and marched forward alone, heading home.

As she forged a path around large granite boulders,

her mind traveled back a few years to when she was twelve. So much had happened since her crowning ceremony. She recalled the events through which she had proven herself worthy, the test of character that had earned her the adorning jewels she now wore with honor. Princess Tiara vowed to never forget the lessons from her siblings and the Old One. Though the conflict with the enemy kingdom destroyed the stables and damaged the Chapel on the Bluffs, the castle itself had been spared.

The Old One told her there would be special seasons as well as difficult ones in life, so she knew a period of rebuilding the Kingdom of Fruitful lay ahead. With a two-hour hike home, Princess Tiara quickened her pace.

CHAPTER 1

THE KINGDOM OF FRUITFUL

In the lore of the Kingdom of Fruitful, stories are told of an old woman making surprise appearances in unexpected places to the royal family. It is said she shows up at significant times to impart wisdom and gifts. Despite her crooked, tiny frame, the Old One moves with surprising speed, using a cane to hobble through the vast acreage of Fruitful. With every unique appearance, her colorful cloak is mentioned. On the most important occasions, the colors of the cape have been known to glow in brilliant mystery.

A self-appointed guardian to the royal family, the peculiar old woman first appeared to King Jonathan and Queen Margaret on their wedding day. Villagers and citizens of nearby kingdoms journeyed to the stately limestone castle, trimmed with simple redwood timber and a modest stone spire. The unassuming castle held beauty deeper than the lovely etchings in its exterior because a virtuous and gracious family resided within. It was no wonder, then, that people were thrilled to attend the betrothal.

After King Jonathan's parents were tragically killed in an accident near the Kingdom of the Rocky Bluffs, he was forced to assume his reign earlier than anticipated. Unmarried at the time, he could no longer delay in choosing a queen. Jonathan wanted a loving partner beside him, so he asked a beloved childhood companion to be his queen. Hailing from the Village of the Pines, Duchess Margaret graciously accepted the proposal. Though long respected by most neighboring empires, the new royal couple inspired deeper admiration for the Kingdom of Fruitful.

Once the long day of ceremony and celebration concluded, the king and queen made their way up the stone stairs of the Great Hall to the elegant marble platform adorned with two gold upholstered oak thrones. The ascent was not for show, however, as guests had already left the festivities. Both king and queen were ready to relax, though it would be the first time they sat next to each other on sovereign thrones.

"I'm warmed by your presence next to me," King Jonathan spoke sincerely, placing his hand in the small of the queen's back to guide her up the stairs. He stepped regally to his throne, his height nearly six inches taller. Intensely focused jade green eyes complemented his dark, mahogany hair. Those eyes now softened into emerald pools as he gazed at his bride.

"Well, I am blessed to be your wife," Queen Margaret said and bowed her head as she ascended the stairs with the grace of a gazelle. Her loose, strawberry blonde curls rested gently on the shoulders of her silk, ivory wedding gown. She raised her head to meet his gaze. Her eyes as crisp as the blue in a cloudless sky twinkled a smile at her debonair husband in his azure surcoat. Once seated, Queen Margaret rested her hand atop the arm of her throne. The king responded to the cue by delicately placing his hand over hers.

Head Servant Joseph smiled broadly as he instructed those putting away the porcelain and crystal. Joseph had dutifully served the royal family for years. He stepped back to study the royal couple on their thrones and considered what lay ahead for the Kingdom of Fruitful. Glancing out the window toward the Mysterious Peaks in the distance, Joseph mused. *These coming years will be a majestic climb to glorious heights, I suspect. I am honored to be here to witness it.*

With all servants occupied, no one noticed a visitor who approached the thrones. Queen Margaret had allowed her eyes to shut for a moment, but they startled open when a quick flash of brilliant color penetrated her closed eyelids. Though the color alerted her, she was not afraid. In fact, a sense of peace filled the hall, causing everyone to pause and investigate the phenomenon. The unique guest wearing a multi-colored cloak wheeled a rickety, cherry wood cart down the red carpet toward the thrones.

At first, Head Servant Joseph stood straight, scanning the Great Hall for danger until he recognized the Old One. No one in the room seemed to notice Joseph's reverent bow as she hobbled past.

Lost in serene expectation of the mysterious ambience, the king and queen eventually realized their visitor kneeled before them at the bottom of the platform. The unsteady cart next to her carried seven gold boxes as well as one large, beige parchment book. She lifted her head, looked directly at the royal couple, and smiled.

King Jonathan shifted his eyes back and forth from the seven gold boxes to the old woman. Queen Margaret stared steadily at the woman's face, studying her expression. Seeing the visitor now struggling to rise, the king immediately descended the stairs to help her stand.

"A king should not bend to his servants, your highness, but I thank you for the assistance," the Old One whispered.

As the king stepped back, she took the seven boxes from her cart. One by one, she carried them closer, carefully laying them along the red carpet at the base of the elevated platform.

Intrigued by the ceremony, Queen Margaret gracefully descended the stairs to be near her husband. Though the stewards stood ready, they sensed the visitor presented no danger, so all watched intently, as a fateful moment for the future of the Kingdom of Fruitful ensued.

"Your highnesses," the guardian stepped back, "I bring you tidings of blessing, and a word of prophecy for the kingdom." Hope filled the air like sunlight saturates morning.

"Go on," King Jonathan squinted, tilting his head and crinkling his brow.

Nodding first to the king and then to the queen, she spoke with authority, "You will bear seven children in the coming years. Two sons and five daughters. These princes and princesses will bring honor to the Kingdom of Fruitful. The people will revere each child, and the royal family will be highly esteemed among neighboring empires."

Queen Margaret gasped at the announcement that she would bear seven children, but quickly resolved herself to a dutiful repose. Understanding she would forever cherish this ordained blessing bestowed upon her unborn children, she cleared her throat, glanced at the king, and promptly grasped his hand.

"Each of these seven boxes carries a crown," the woman stated as her arm spanned the display. "However, before each child receives their crown, they must endure a test of character. All seven princes and princesses will demonstrate strength of virtue, proven by how they overcome a challenging situation. The jewels in their crowns will be determined by the virtue demonstrated."

The Old One returned to her cart to retrieve the large, beige parchment book bound with brown leather strips. An imprint of an olive tree and dove decorated the front cover. She carried the book to the royal couple, extending it for them to see. With one hand underneath, the wrinkled fingers from her free hand traced the design on the cover as she spoke.

"This is the *Book of Truth*. Within its pages are blessings for the Kingdom of Fruitful. As king and queen, you must read the words herein faithfully and often. As you do, you will discover verses for your children that consecrate their unique virtue. Every crowning ceremony will include a reading of each prince and princess's blessing."

At that, the woman bowed slightly, her hands still holding the heavy parchment. As she lifted her head, she extended her arms and placed the book into the king's hands. Like a misty fog, a mysterious awe enveloped the entire Great Hall. Led by Head Servant Joseph, all witnessing the prophecy kneeled.

King Jonathan placed the *Book of Truth* upon an alabaster stand nearby and stepped toward the Old One. "We thank and honor you, kind woman. Tell us who you are. By what name shall we call you?"

"You may call me *Old One*, your highness, for I am a simple servant sent to be your guardian." She curtsied briefly, then lifted her eyes heavenward. A smile brightened her expression as she spoke less formally, "You will see me again, my lord, my lady. A guardian continually keeps watch over her charges. You will not always be aware of my presence; however, I will appear at each child's crowning ceremony to proclaim the blessing from the *Book of Truth*."

With that, she grabbed the rickety cart in one hand, her cane in the other, and hobbled back down the red carpet with surprising speed. The king and queen watched in wonder. What they saw next confirmed they had been in the presence of the supernatural. Like the aurora borealis, the colors of her cape glowed in emanating beauty again. Not a quick flash of color like before, but a sustained radiance that only faded after the Old One was gone.

CHAPTER 2

FOREST FUN

(YEARS LATER)

"Ugh," Princess Tiara complained to the waddling ducks along the grassy bank of Singing Creek. Directly addressing a nearby mallard, she grimaced, "It's already time to head back to the castle for dinner." Kicking up leaves, she took one last look around Forest Valley, hoping to find a distraction to delay the inevitable.

Suddenly, as the twelve-year-old princess scanned the panorama, a bright, colorful flash shone behind a large elm tree in the path ahead. It disappeared as quickly as it came. *That's odd. I'm certain I saw a similar flash just last week when I hiked near the Cave of Stones. Could there be a new animal in our kingdom that I'm unaware of? A bird of rare color perhaps?*

Just the diversion she needed, Tiara jogged in the

direction of the tree chased by bunnies and squirrels, scolding each other along the way. She found nothing unique once she stopped at the tree. Panting, she brushed her long, brown hair out of her hazel-green eyes and straightened her light blue tunic. She stood quietly, wondering if she should have worn her hair up in a bun that day. *No*, she corrected herself, *I can feel the forest's freedom better when I wear my hair down.*

Slowly turning 360 degrees, she refocused her curiosity, still looking for a mystery. "This *is* the right tree. This *is* where I saw the flash." The princess rested against a rock, bending down to pet Socky, her favorite forest cat who had meandered in her direction. The four white paws against his black fur helped her choose his name. Socky rubbed against her leg as she listened to his soothing purr. A soft, twilight breeze caused her to button her grey corduroy cape as she breathed in the woodsy air. How she loved this forest and its animals.

Scratching behind Socky's ears, Tiara spoke her thoughts aloud, "Why can't I fully enjoy being part of the royal family? Mother and Father look at me with such disappointment lately. They keep talking about princess-like behavior. I can tell they do not think I demonstrate anything close to it."

She picked up the cat to set him on her lap, but he squirmed, so she let him jump down. "You must feel the same way I do when I am told to be *dignified*. We just want to be free, don't we?"

The young princess's eyes traveled to the castle in the distance as she stood to leave the sanctuary of the forest. Her thoughts turned inward. *The worry on their faces constantly reminds me that I have not yet proven myself worthy of wearing a crown. I simply do not want to think about it. I dread that silly crowning ceremony. It is just needless fanfare. What's special about wearing a heavy crown anyway?*

Feeling anxious, she resolved to cease this line of thought. She turned and spoke aloud again to all the nearby animals, "No matter. It will all work out somehow. I might dread the crowning ceremony, whenever it happens, but I do love my family. My older siblings are truly kind and fun to be with. It is a blessing to be a part of this kingdom."

Glancing around the forest's panorama once more, she raised both arms and finished her soliloquy, "The best part of being a princess is freely exploring these lovely woods, hiking up grassy hills, and resting in quiet meadows. I will prove myself soon enough to get my crown. However, I shall not worry about it today!"

She smiled to see one or two animals still watching her, as they seemed to empathize with her situation. Catching sight of a deer behind a bush where a few meadowlarks kept their distance near Singing Creek, Tiara sighed pensively at the peaceful scene. It was one of nature's precious paintings.

The sun was now lowering behind rolling hills, and Tiara grabbed her satchel. *Yikes! I'm going to be late for dinner again. Father and Mother will be quite upset.* "Keep an eye out for more color flashes, will you?" she yelled to the faraway deer. *I really need to figure out why I am seeing them. What if we actually have a new animal friend roaming the forest?* With that, Princess Tiara ran at full speed back to the castle.

When the young princess was out of sight, the deer gracefully turned to face an old woman dressed in a bright, colorful cloak and resting against a large boulder several yards down the flower-filled riverbank. A strange radiance surrounded her, brightening the serenity of the forest scene.

CHAPTER 3

LATE AGAIN

"I'm sorry I'm late," Princess Tiara announced, bowing her head upon entering the formal dining room. Having quickly finger-combed her hair, several tangled ends betrayed her haste. Her beige dinner gown fit oddly crooked at the top. With quick alternating glances from her mother's side of the large, oak table to her father's, she continued acknowledging her shortcoming. "Mother, Father, please forgive me. I know this is not the first time I have been late. I realize my behavior does not reflect the dignity of royalty."

The air was thick with silence, and the oval-shaped table seemed larger than usual as she pulled out her high back chair between Princess Grace and Prince Joshua. Tiara's heart sank to see her mother's eyes lower. *She can't even look me in the eye*, she condemned herself, refusing to glance at the king.

As the princess sat down, Prince Joshua purposefully leaned his broad shoulders into hers with a friendly side-shove. Slowly bending forward, he stealthily turned his head her way, and catching her eyes, he winked. Tiara widened her eyes and mouthed, "sorry," then smiled at the gesture that forgave her tardiness.

On her other side, Princess Grace was more direct. Tilting her head and crinkling her nose, she studied Tiara's appearance. Her agate green eyes sparkled against dark, copper hair. Soon her face brightened with a broad smile. Stifling a chuckle, Grace brushed off tiny twigs and grasses from Tiara's shoulders. Then she scooted her chair out to stand behind her younger sister and rebutton the poorly fitting gown.

Tiara breathed in the support of her siblings as Princess Lauren leaned her way to whisper, "We're glad you're here, safe and sound, Tiara."

Returning Lauren's smile, Tiara finally felt brave enough to look at her parents again. The king summoned a servant to bring her dinner plate, while the queen dabbed the corners of her mouth with a grey linen napkin. Tiara looked across the table at Princess Desiree, dressed in a coral gown, sitting tall and straight against the carved high back walnut chair. Desiree returned her gaze with twinkling purity. Next to Desiree, Tiara's eyes moved to Prince Burton Kenson (nicknamed B.K.), who gazed up at the ceiling, seemingly unaware of her late arrival. His brown hickory vest offset his almond eyes. Since he was always deep in thought, Tiara was not sure Prince B.K. even noticed she was late.

It was Princess Brittani who spoke confidently to break the awkward silence. Eager to hear about Tiara's experiences, Brittani leaned forward from across the table to ask, "What kept you out this long, Tiara? Tell us about your adventures today." Surprisingly, Prince B.K. quickly abandoned his contemplation, eagerly fixing his eyes on Tiara. *Maybe he does pay attention*, she wondered. Tiara glanced nervously from the king to the queen before speaking.

"Well... uh... I was playing with the animals in the forest, of course. I played with Socky a bit. I even saw a deer several yards away. Also, there was this brief flash of bright color in the distance. I've seen it before, too, near the Cave of Stones. I can't seem to figure out if it's a new animal or what."

Tiara's last comment brought instant reaction from everyone. Almost immediately, Queen Margaret widened her eyes and raised her eyebrows, looking directly at the king. Lauren and Grace exchanged knowing smiles. Brittani cupped her hand over her opened mouth, while Desiree and Joshua grinned as they looked down at their plates. Tiara noticed Prince B.K. lean back in his chair again, gazing heavenward, his mouth twisted.

Tiara wanted to ask about this collective response but hesitated. She had caused enough trouble already and was not eager to bring any additional attention to herself. The rest of dinner was generally quiet. Tiara stopped chewing once or twice to give more thought to her family's reaction, for none had even replied to her comment. Did they all know something about this flash of bright color? What were they keeping from her?

Once dinner was over, Tiara grabbed Princess Grace by the hand. As they made their way to the top of the maple staircase, Tiara heard whispering below. She leaned over the wooden railing and looked down to the vestibule where her parents carried on an animated conversation. King Jonathan cupped his chin thoughtfully, stroking his beard while holding Queen Margaret's wrist with his free hand. With flashing eyes, the queen waved her free arm. She was visibly concerned, a manner the girls had not seen before.

Tiara could not hear their words but observed her father doing all he could to reassure his wife.

Stepping back from the railing, she turned to her sister. "This is not normal, Grace. They never act this way. Mother is visibly upset. Look at her!" Tiara placed her hands on her hips. "Are you going to tell me what's going on?"

Lacing her arm through Tiara's extended elbow, Grace guided Tiara to the doors of their adjacent bed chambers. She hugged her close, then held her at arm's length. "Don't worry, Little 'T.' This is good, I promise. Mother may look upset, but she is also excited about what is to come. She probably just needs time to think it through, just like you will in the near future. Something special will happen soon. You must be patient. Now, how about we check on Oscar, your chinchilla? He has been in his cage all day. I'm sure he's missed you and is eager to play."

CHAPTER 4

ANNOUNCING THE PLAN

Witnessing her parents' passionate conversation in the vestibule after dinner caused Princess Tiara to toss and turn in angst all night. As the sun rose, she reluctantly forced herself to dress appropriately for the day, fully expecting the king to call a meeting to issue a proclamation relating to the dignity required from princesses, and her lack of demonstrating it. Despite her siblings' graciousness at dinner, she assumed her parents were upset with her tardiness.

It was little surprise, then, when a steward knocked on the bed chamber door early the next morning with the announcement of a meeting in the Great Hall. At the first tap on the door, Tiara swung it open ready to face what could no longer be avoided. Dressed in a maroon gown with a pearl bodice, she nodded acknowledgement to the servant as he gave her the written note with the time and purpose for the meeting.

Tiara grabbed her quill pen and parchment papers, unsure of what to expect. She placed some hay and carrots in Oscar's cage. "I can't resist any longer, Oscar. I don't know what will be required of me after today, but I must be brave and face whatever it is I'm asked to do." Like a minstrel changing tunes, she then smiled at the chinchilla, "I'll fill you in on all the details when I return."

As Tiara latched the bed chamber door, a bright flash of color caught her eye at the end of the hall near the top of the staircase. Immediately, Princess Tiara pushed past the servant, now knocking on Princess Grace's door.

Before she could get too far, Princess Desiree hurried beside her. Rushing to pull her long, blonde hair into a bun, Desiree quickly adjusted her lavender gown. She strategically positioned herself in Tiara's path.

"You are in quite a hurry this morning, Tiara. Is everything all right?"

"Oh, g-g-good m-m-morning, Desiree. I...ah...I need to go somewhere quickly before the announcement. I need to investigate something I just saw."

Desiree guided wisely, "Why don't I accompany you to help then? Two sets of eyes are better than one; besides, we must not be late for the meeting. Tell me just what it is I should be looking for?"

"Well," Tiara resisted the urge to run off after the light but turned to explain. "It's...It's that burst of color again. I just saw it flash at the top of the staircase, and now it's gone. It can't be an animal, can it? Head Servant Joseph would not allow any creature loose inside the castle. I must figure out where this rapid flash of color comes from and why I keep seeing it."

Desiree walked briskly at Tiara's side. Allowing her long legs to keep up with Tiara's hurried pace, she descended the stairs quickly enough to get in front of Tiara by the time they'd reached the bottom. Just before Tiara rushed out the castle entrance, Desiree grabbed her hands.

"You must trust me now, sister. We need to go to the Great Hall for the proclamation. Your curiosity is delightful, but I am nearly certain you'll find some answers this morning. I cannot promise you will fully understand these flashes of color yet, however I can promise the purpose will be revealed soon."

Not wanting to refuse her oldest sister's counsel,

Tiara stood still. With the slightest furrow in her brow, she forced herself to look into Desiree's cobalt blue eyes—eyes with the queen's same sparkle. As she met her sister's assuring gaze, her tightened shoulders fell, and an acquiescing breath indicated compliance.

Lowering her head slightly, Tiara sighed. "Well, I have no choice but to trust you. Princess Grace gave me similar assurance last night. I do wish you all would be more forthcoming with whatever secret you are keeping."

With a hearty laugh, Princess Desiree grabbed Tiara's hand. "Come now, sis. Let's join the others to find out exactly what mother and father are thinking."

Together they headed to the Great Hall to line up as protocol demanded. In formal procession down the red carpet, oldest to youngest, they reached the elevated platform where the king and queen awaited on their thrones. Six of the seven children wore crowns, the importance of the announcement enhanced by the sparkling gems in the center of each diadem. Tiara wiggled nervously, sensing all eyes on her. She was certain they could hear her knees knocking.

The king rose. "Good morning, children. I trust you slept well. Seeing you wearing your crowns always brings Mother and me immense pride. However, as you know, our youngest does not yet wear her crown."

Though she desperately wanted to turn and bolt out of the beloved ballroom, Tiara forced herself to stand tall and look directly at the king. Burying her trepidation, she reassured herself with the knowledge that each of her siblings also faced this same moment in their childhood.

Queen Margaret now stood to take her place next to the king.

"Tiara, we know this long-awaited crowning has caused a bit of anxiety for you." The queen's more tender gaze helped Tiara settle. "Your free spirit and love of adventure is part of who you are. You must know your family cherishes and appreciates your need to explore our lovely kingdom."

With a hopeful smile, Tiara nodded as the queen continued.

"You must not think wearing a crown will take away from your fondness for nature. However, it is time for you to earn the jewel for your crown so you can wear it as proudly as your siblings wear theirs. You possess a virtue of character just as they do. Now you must discover what that virtue is. No one in this room knows. We are all quite eager to find out."

Another breath of anticipation filled Tiara's lungs as the king stepped forward to issue the proclamation.

"Princess Tiara, to help you feel more comfortable with your upcoming crowning, we have decided you will spend the next six days accompanied by another prince or princess. Each morning one will greet you and determine activities for the day. There is a purpose in this. At some point in your time together, your siblings will explain to you the challenge they experienced that proved them worthy to wear their crown. The gems their crowns hold reflect the virtue they demonstrated when their character was tested. It is our intention that as you learn from your siblings, you will become more..." the king hesitated.

"It is our hope," the queen stepped forward to assist, "that you will come to understand the wonderful virtue of character your delightful personality is fitted to."

The king's nod acknowledged his gratitude for the queen's positive wording.

And so, it was.

And so, it came to be.

Princess Tiara would spend the next six days learning from her siblings.

Chapter 5

Amethyst

The next morning, Tiara woke to see Princess Desiree opening the bed chamber's ivory curtains. "Good morning, sweet sister. Are you ready to spend the day together?"

Tiara threw off the maroon quilted blanket, jumped out of bed and ran toward Desiree. She hugged the oldest princess without hesitation.

"Your enthusiasm is like the bright sunshine coming through this window." Desiree cupped Tiara's face lovingly. "You seem very excited."

"Well, I'm happy to see you, of course, but I'm not sure I'm eager to spend so many days thinking about what virtue I have."

Princess Desiree took Tiara's hand, "Yes, I understand. Remember, we've all been through a time of discovering our virtue. I can understand why you might be apprehensive."

Together they looked out the window at the kingdom's rolling hills, Desiree's tall frame sheltering her sister. Desiree released her hand and gently rested her arm on Tiara's shoulder. The young princess's eyes were drawn to the deep purple amethyst in the center of her sister's crown. It highlighted Desiree's flaxen blonde hair. She stared at the gem and wondered what she would learn about how the amethyst was earned.

"I see you are studying my crown," Desiree remarked. "Don't worry too much about my story yet. Let's just enjoy our day together for a while, okay?"

Unsure of what to do next, Tiara moved to the armoire to dress, while Desiree strode elegantly over to straighten the bed. Observing her sister's graceful walk, Tiara became aware of her own awkwardness. Mesmerized by the elegance, she froze as her hazel eyes studied every step. She shook herself back into focus, but as she dressed, Tiara tried to mimic the same calm stature. Holding her head high, she walked with longer than normal steps to the mirror. Suddenly distracted at the sight of Oscar, her chinchilla, however, Tiara immediately lost interest in walking gracefully.

"Princess Desiree," she squealed, "don't forget to

greet Oscar." She opened the door to the cage to let her pet roam the room.

"Of course! Good morning, Oscar Chinchilla! How are you today?"

Desiree bent to scratch the animal's silvery fur, while Tiara beamed to see the interaction. Plopping down on the floor, she lifted Oscar into her arms and sat on the ottoman near the cage. Tiara explained that chinchillas can live to be twenty years old and are able to make ten different vocalizations. She went on to note that though they can survive cold temperatures, they should not remain in places higher than eighty degrees Fahrenheit.

By this time, Desiree sat cross-legged on the stone floor near the cage, listening intently.

"You have taught me much, Tiara. I am always impressed by your knowledge of animals."

"Thank you. I love learning about them. I especially enjoy observing their natural habitat."

Desiree pulled herself up to a stand, straightened the pearl decorated bodice of her periwinkle tunic and adjusted her crown. "Well then, I suspect we should spend our time together today outside, shouldn't we?"

"Yes! I was hoping you'd want to do some hiking. Might we go to the same place I was two days ago in Forest Valley? It's in the clearing near Singing Creek.

There were many animals there. I'd like to see if the deer I encountered is still near the riverbank."

"It sounds lovely and like a wonderful place to talk as well."

Tiara grimaced as she brushed her wavy brown hair, examining herself in the glass mirror atop the armoire. *I hope the conversation about virtue is quick so we can spend more time looking for the deer.* She kept her thoughts to herself as she put on a light grey cape over her pale-yellow tunic.

Once ready, they headed down the staircase, Tiara's eyes fixed on Desiree, mesmerized by her older sister's graceful manner. Head Servant Joseph waited at the castle entrance, bowing slightly as he opened the large bronze door for the princesses. He watched, smiling, as they strolled down the terraced gardens and across the lush green grass before closing the door.

Soon the two sisters arrived at the Meadow of Hyacinths where Tiara stopped to tighten the laces on her boots. Princess Desiree purposefully asked questions about various flowers, giving Tiara opportunity to point out several blooms ready to open.

"Our kingdom is so lovely, isn't it?" Desiree twirled, swinging her arms like a child. Surprised by this loss of decorum, Tiara joined in right away, soon flopping down in the tall grasses. *This is far more fun than I thought it would be,* she mused. *Princess Desiree may be graceful and dignified, but she also knows how to play.* Eventually the two princesses crossed the wooden bridge over Singing Creek, reaching Tiara's favorite section of Forest Valley.

"Let me show you the elm tree where I saw the flash of color and noticed the deer." Tiara moved ahead, then hesitated briefly. She attempted walking elegantly again. However, when she noticed a bunny hopping her way, she abandoned the attempt to be graceful and ran after the rabbit. Quite amused by this, Desiree joined in the chase which thrilled the youngest princess.

After looking for the deer awhile, they concluded it was nowhere nearby. Desiree leaned against a sturdy branch of the elm while Tiara decided to search for Socky, her favorite cat. As she relaxed, Desiree caught sight of a bright and colorful cape behind a hibiscus bush down along the creekbank. A wrinkled face peeked around the side of the bush and winked. Desiree acknowledged the Old One with a nod and a smile.

"Tiara," she called, "Why don't you join me? I believe it's time to tell you the story of how I earned the amethyst for my crown."

Though she did not want to stop exploring, she knew this was the purpose of their day together. Tiara walked obediently to the tree and nestled herself in the curve of a large limb next to Desiree.

Noting her sister's reluctance, Desiree reached over and patted her hand. "I think you'll enjoy this story once you hear it." Tiara's nod signaled interest, so Desiree continued.

"When I was just thirteen, only a year older than you are now, Father appointed me to be Child Ambassador to the neighboring kingdoms. The purpose for the assignment was to build relationships with children of other empires. It meant that I traveled regularly in a carriage escorted by a coachman. I often visited the Kingdom of Grassy Plains, the Kingdom of Solstice, and the Kingdom of Rocky Bluffs."

"Did you ever go to the Kingdom of Mysterious Peaks?" Tiara interrupted.

"No. Father did not wish to stir up any suspicions that could result in conflict with them. Father says no one should visit that kingdom without a regimen of soldiers. Don't you know that Tiara?"

"Yes, I know." Tiara hung her head. "But I do hope to journey there someday. No one really knows what kind of animals live in those mountains. And I am almost certain that the source of water for Singing Creek comes from high in the peaks."

While Princess Desiree pondered the unexpected course the conversation was taking, Tiara continued. "Head Servant Joseph told me the people of that kingdom are not like us. I sure would like to discover more about them. Can you tell me what you know?"

Desiree straightened herself to a sturdier stance, moving away from the tree and facing Tiara.

"Well, no one really knows if the people from the Kingdom of Mysterious Peaks are like us, but they are certainly unfamiliar to us. Many people speculate they are from a faraway country and migrated to those high mountains for some reason. Head Servant Joseph knows much more than I do. Perhaps we should find time to speak with him. I'm sorry I don't know more."

"That's a wonderful idea, Desiree. If we find out more from Head Servant Joseph, maybe Father will reconsider allowing us to visit and explore. That would be amazing."

Desiree laughed. "Yes, it would. For now, however, we'd better continue considering what virtue will earn you a crown."

Tiara's expression fell back into focus.

"I think you will become more enthusiastic about your crowning ceremony in a few days, after you spend time with us. Think of your virtue as a large boulder near a lovely riverbank. You can rest safely on top of its sturdiness and still absorb the beauty that surrounds you."

Dutifully, Tiara lowered her head and focused more intently.

"Anyway, my first trip was to the Kingdom of Solstice, one of the farthest away empires. It was to be a long day of travel. Coachman Klaus was assigned to drive the carriage. As we rode along, I became aware that Klaus turned on a narrow, dirt road, veering off the kingdom highways. When I inquired as to why he took a detour, he informed me he'd discovered a way to avoid paying the expensive highway tolls imposed on all travelers who sought to enter the Kingdom of Solstice."

Tiara giggled, "That's sneaky, isn't it? From what I know about Coachman Klaus, he would try to cut corners for sure. He's kind of creepy, don't you think?"

"Well," Desiree spoke directly, "I did not find Klaus's rule-breaking at all funny. He was quite nonchalant about violating agreements with neighboring kingdoms. I ordered him to stop, but he pretended not to hear. With as loud a voice as I could muster, I told him we must honor the laws of other empires. I knew he heard me, but he simply shrugged his shoulders and whipped the horses to go faster."

Tiara sat up and gasped, "That is very disrespectful. Klaus is not at all like Head Servant Joseph or Stableman Kegan, is he? How did you react to his disregard?"

"I stood up in the carriage and reached for the reigns, ordering Coachman Klaus to turn around. He had to stop when I rose, but the look on his face was not at all pleased. I insisted he travel on the authorized highway. He knew he had to obey. Once we arrived in the Kingdom of the Solstice, however, he did not even help me out of the carriage, nor accompany me into their palace as he is supposed to.

"Later, after we returned from the trip, I told Father what happened. He reprimanded Klaus and re-instructed him in protocols to follow for travel. Coachman Klaus refused to chauffeur my carriage anywhere again."

Tiara furrowed her brow and pursed her lips as she processed the story. "You were very brave. Especially since no one would have known whether you used the dirt roads or not. It would have been easier to just let it go, don't you think?"

"Easier, yes, but not honorable. Sometimes the easy thing to do is NOT the right thing to do. We can only imagine where Klaus's lack of respect might have led if I hadn't corrected him. His compromising and reckless attitude may have marred the reputation of our kingdom. To maintain our long history of living peacefully with our neighbors, we must honor their rules." Desiree leaned forward against an outward-curving branch, lowering her eyes to study Tiara's reaction.

"I understand," Tiara replied succinctly, nervously aware of her older sister's convictions. "Is this confrontation you had with Coachman Klaus how you earned your amethyst?"

"Yes. This amethyst stands for the *virtue of righteousness*. It is a constant reminder to make the right choice, no matter how convenient it may be to choose an easier way."

Desiree went on to explain that once the king and queen confirmed her firm stance with Klaus, they scheduled her crowning ceremony, for she had proven herself virtuous. Her face beamed as she explained more, "The most special part of the day was when they pulled out the *Book of Truth* and read my blessing."

Tiara tilted her head, squinting. "Wait. What's the *Book of Truth*?"

"Oh dear, I guess you don't know about the *Book of Truth* yet. Perhaps I wasn't supposed to tell you."

Tiara climbed out of her perch on the branch and stomped away. "Augh!" She raised her arms and turned to face her sister. "This is another example of how everyone keeps secrets. No one thought to tell me about this *Book of Truth*. None of you seem to want me to understand the flash of colorful light either. I'm just supposed to figure everything out by myself." She paced over to a rock and plopped down, "Will you please tell me about the *Book of Truth* since you brought it up?"

Desiree reached her arms out and motioned for Tiara to come to her. Near tears, Tiara ran to her arms, receiving her older sister's hug. "Sweet sister, we don't want to overwhelm you with too much information all at once. Let's just take each of the coming days one at a time. For now, we'll talk about the blessing I received from the *Book of Truth*. You'll understand more as you spend time with your other siblings, okay?"

She gently held Tiara at arm's length. Tiara sniffed, keeping her eyes on Desiree.

"My blessing is extremely meaningful to me. I recite it every day. Are you ready? '*The path of the righteous is like the light of dawn, which shines brighter and brighter until full day' (Proverbs 4:18 ESV).*"

A hint of a smile brightened Tiara's expression. Hearing the lovely words of blessing lifted her mood, and she immediately relaxed, pondering the picture of early morning that Desiree's blessing painted. Desiree's countenance did shine like the sunrise in the morning sky. It was true that most people of the kingdom respected Princess Desiree. In fact, throughout the land, she was known as *the righteous princess*.

Tiara climbed back onto the branch, and the sisters rested silently for several minutes. Desiree took off her crown, handing it to Tiara. She purposefully gave Tiara time to contemplate.

Princess Tiara gazed at the lovely amethyst. Soon, her eyes moved to focus on the beauty of the forest. She imagined herself in the position of ambassador to other kingdoms. It would provide amazing opportunities to study landscapes and learn about animals. There would be complex decisions in that role requiring her to have integrity with every action. Saying and doing the right thing would be critical. She may have to stand up to difficult people like Coachman Klaus, but it would also give her the chance to explore the Kingdom of Mysterious Peaks if she could convince her father to allow it.

Is it possible, she wondered, gently touching the amethyst, *that my virtue might also be the virtue of righteousness*? She envisioned herself wearing a crown with an amethyst in the center, walking with dignity like Princess Desiree. Her daydream gave her a sense of pride and stirred unfamiliar curiosity.

As Tiara pondered, she realized she was not completely resentful of her upcoming crowning. In fact, she had a growing sense of anticipation. The importance of making the right decision despite having easier choices intrigued her. Her pensive moments vanished quickly, however, when she noticed squirrels digging at the base of the tree. In no time at all, Tiara convinced Princess Desiree to help her gather special grasses to take home to Oscar.

CHAPTER 6

RHODOCHROSITE

Princess Tiara skipped through the parapet walk heading to the northwest corner tower. Princess Brittani designated this as their meeting spot at dinner the night before and waited for Tiara. Brittani grinned at the youngest princess as she approached, golden blonde shoulder-length hair enhancing her bubbly smile. Tiara squealed to see her sister at the end of the parapet walk. Brittani intentionally wore her crown, bejeweled with a sparkling pink rhodochrosite in the center.

Noticing the glisten, Tiara found herself giggling as she recalled a trick she often played on villagers. Because the rhodochrosite shone vibrantly, especially outside, people sometimes mistakenly thought the sun became extra bright when Brittani walked by. These noticeable reactions from villagers amused Tiara, so she regularly found ways to convince her sister to visit villages on sunny days just to see heads turn, eyes pop, and smiles spread. Brittani never minded Tiara's trickery, however, because she adored being among the people of the kingdom.

Tiara stopped abruptly when she saw Brittani dressed in riding clothes. She slapped her hand against the side of her head. "Oh dear. Are we going riding today?"

"Absolutely, we are riding today. Didn't I mention that at dinner?" Princess Brittani asked.

Tiara swung her head back and stomped a foot. "I forgot. Can I run back and redress?"

"Of course. I'll walk with you. As we walk, I want to ask you a question about what you said at dinner the day you arrived late from the forest?"

In rapid fire, Tiara's eyes raced side to side as she tried to remember her comments from that uncomfortable evening. "Uh...what did I say?"

"You were talking about seeing the flash of color in the forest. You briefly mentioned you'd seen the same phenomenon at the Cave of Stones."

Immediately, Tiara's demeanor sunk. She slowed her pace and hung her head. "Oh yes... Uh... I hoped no one heard that. I know we are not supposed to go near the Cave of Stones without permission. Do you think Mother and Father were aware of my comment? If they were, I'm pretty sure I would have been reprimanded right then and there."

"I agree. Had they really heard your comment, you would have known by now."

Once inside Tiara's bed chamber, Brittani walked directly to Oscar's cage to pick him up. If any of her siblings enjoyed nature the way Tiara did, it was Princess Brittani, who adored studying landscapes, and learning about plant and animal life. Scratching Oscar's ears, Brittani glanced sideways at her sister. Then a mischievous smile spread across her face as she hurried over to Tiara's closet to help find riding clothes.

"Sweet sister, you know how I also love exploring, right? You and I have had wonderful adventures together, learning all we can about nature. I understand the temptation to investigate the cave. There are hundreds of creatures, various kinds of rock, unique plant life, and possible hidden streams of water inside, right?"

With eyes widening, Tiara wiggled in excitement to think of the love for knowledge she and Brittani shared. "Yes! Then you know why I went there. I just could not resist the idea. I did not go inside the cave, I promise. There were sentries posted at the entrance anyway. They would never have let me go in. I did ask a guard to accompany me inside, but of course, he refused."

Brittani laughed, "Yes. I did the same thing a few years ago. The sentries refused me as well. It is frustrating, I know." Brittani took off her crown, sweeping her long hair to the side. "I'm wondering something. When you said you saw a flash of color, did it come from inside the cave?"

"I'm not sure, exactly. It was extremely fast. It could have come from inside. I asked the guards if they noticed it. Do you know what they said?" Tiara did not wait for Brittani to respond. "They told me to go home!"

Tiara frowned and walked away from the closet to sit on her bed. She rested her elbows on her legs and plopped her head down upon her open hands.

Brittani sat next to her, placing a hand on her shoulder. "Well, I have a surprise for you today, little sister. We are going to ride to the Cave of Stones! I got permission from Father."

"What? Are you serious?" Tiara flew back across the room to the closet, pushing clothes around until she found her riding outfit. Pulling on brown breeches and paddock boots, she shrieked, "This is wonderful!"

She threw on a tan chemisette and grabbed her grey surcoat. "Oh, we'd better take some parchment and ink to jot down what we observe inside the cave."

"Wait a minute, young lady." Brittani buttoned Tiara's surcoat. "You know we cannot go all the way inside. We only have permission to step into the cave and observe from the entrance. However, I am bringing a lamp we can use to shine on areas we want to see more clearly!" Brittani bent forward laughing, "Let's get going!"

The two princesses ran down the stairs and out the door with a quick wave to Head Servant Joseph. They jogged around the castle to the stables. Approximately five-hundred feet behind them, hobbling as fast as she could, the Old One tried to keep up. Glancing back, Brittani noticed her. She smiled at the mysterious guardian, realizing the pink in the cape seemed extra vibrant this day. The Old One breathed heavily, so Brittani intentionally paused in the Meadow of Hyacinths to pick bluebells. This enthused and distracted Tiara, allowing the old woman to sneak around them.

Once on the path again, the princesses reached the stables in minutes. They asked Kegan, the stableman, for two saddled horses. Tiara could not help but notice Princess Brittani returning Kegan's nod with a flirtatious smile. She wondered if there might be a fondness developing between them. While Tiara mulled over the possibility, Princess Brittani leaned against the fence, took off her crown, and pointed to the beautiful rhodochrosite. Tiara sat down on a large boulder nearby.

"Tiara, I know you love to trick me into 'showing off' the sparkle of this jewel to the people of the kingdom, but I want to tell you about the challenge I experienced that allows me the privilege of wearing this bright gem."

Tiara's mouth dropped open, "I didn't know you knew about my playing tricks. Perhaps I should apologize." She laughed. "It's quite fun to see the reaction of the villagers, however. The rhodochrosite is extremely radiant, more than any other gemstone. It must symbolize the brightest virtue. What does it represent?"

Princess Brittani explained to Tiara the rhodochrosite stood for the *virtue of knowledge*. Brittani's love of people instilled a sincere desire to know more about them. She continually asked questions of whomever she met. *How did you learn this? What does this task accomplish? What do you believe causes this?* She genuinely wanted to understand. She developed an enormous bank of knowledge by questioning people. This inquisitive practice filled her with a thirst for discovery. In fact, schoolteachers would often invite her to teach a lesson to their students. Sometimes, teachers would ask Brittani instead of the kingdom's sages and advisors.

Brittani's expression grew somber, "Because teachers invited me to speak, the sages and advisors grew jealous. I guess they worried their role in the kingdom might change. Perhaps they feared the king and queen might seek counsel from me instead of them."

Seeds of jealousy festered in the minds of the sages like the stubborn root of an ugly thistle. Before long they conspired against Brittani, developing a scheme to prove her knowledge was less than their own. A sinister plan in place, they summoned the princess to appear for questioning at Cornucopia Village town hall. Intrigued by the order, she went eagerly, curious to know why they wished to interrogate her.

"As soon as I arrived," Brittani recounted, "I realized I had fallen prey to a deceptive ploy. Set up like a courtroom, I sat on one side of a large table while all the sages faced me from the other side. Their scowls revealed anger as they fired one question after another. I barely had time to think."

Tiara stared wide-eyed, "You must have been scared. Did you feel threatened?"

"I was nervous at first, but after three or four questions aimed like arrows, I began to enjoy the challenge. Though I realized their motivations were suspect, I decided to play along. I answered nearly every question correctly. They challenged me with accusations: *Did you know this*? Or *Did you realize that*? They were clearly trying to prove my knowledge of certain topics was only surface level.

"In the end, I stumped several of the advisors by telling them more than *they* knew about certain topics. I didn't intend to cause resentment. I wanted to demonstrate that the pursuit of knowledge is a worthy quest for anyone, not just sages and advisors. Honestly, Tiara, it was exhilarating."

Though Brittani had answered each question with poise, the sages became indignant, and continued to devise plans rooted in envy. The insidious jealousy eventually caused them to refuse to speak with the princess whenever she tried to converse.

"It saddened me because I always enjoyed the intellectual discussions we'd previously engaged in. When they stopped talking to me, I told Father."

Once wise to their scheme, King Jonathan suspended each sage. He appointed Princess Brittani to the role of advisor instead. It was as if they had set themselves up for what they feared the most. However, Princess Brittani didn't agree with her father.

"I did not want to refuse Father, but it didn't feel fair to suspend the advisors. They truly are brilliant people. The ugliness of envy caused them to lose sight of true wisdom. I told Father we must celebrate their knowledge. I asked him to reinstate them."

Tiara stood up to face her sister, "I'm surprised you defended them. They were not at all showing wisdom in scheming to make you look simple. You are a princess. They should never have plotted against you in that way."

"Correct, little sister. It is a perfect example of how foolish a person full of knowledge can become when they let jealousy capture their thoughts. Knowledge must unite with kindness and patience. It can never be possessed by just a few. All the facts, all the research, all the learning we love is meant to be shared. It does not matter who is the most intelligent. It is far more important to teach each other what we know."

"Tell me how this situation was resolved. I know you are not an advisor; therefore, father must have changed his mind."

Brittani explained that with her encouragement, the king recommissioned the sages and advisors.

However, he commanded them to collaborate with her to help citizens become more informed. A new proclamation created special conferences where villagers could learn a variety of disciplines. Soon, the sages and advisors were so enthralled in the development of these courses they forgot about their jealousies. Brittani intentionally asked them many questions, once again charming them into sharing their knowledge.

"The joy of seeing others learn brought back an appreciation for discovery. The educational forums became extremely popular." Princess Brittani spread her arms out as if trying to capture the air.

Tiara now understood why Brittani was known throughout the kingdom as *the intelligent princess.* "Wonderful!" Tiara cheered, climbing on top of the fence to sit next to her sister. "I think I know what my gem is going to be! Since I love knowledge as much as you do, I'm certain I will receive the rhodochrosite in my crown, too."

Brittani beamed, placing her crown atop Tiara's head. "Maybe," she laughed as the crown slid down one side. "Remember, you still have much to learn from the rest of your siblings. Do not rush knowledge, little sister. Just inhale it steadily like fresh morning air."

"How did you feel at your crowning?" Tiara inquired, adjusting her sister's crown which slid down her head again.

"It was incredibly special. Even though crowning ceremonies are only for the royal family, Father and Mother thought it would be appropriate to invite the advisors and sages, too. They were extremely respectful. None of them had heard a blessing from the *Book of Truth* before."

Tiara jumped hastily off the fence, handing the crown back to Brittani. She placed her hands on her hips, her forehead creased. "Again, with that *Book of Truth*! No one has explained it to me. What is this *Book of Truth*?"

"Hmm... I don't think you are supposed to completely understand it until your own crowning ceremony. But I can tell you that along with your jewel, you will also receive a blessing. It is a saying of promise for your future. Do you want to know what my blessing was?"

Tiara's frustration melted with Brittani's encouragement for patience. She relaxed her arms and stepped back toward the fence, "Yes, I do. But if we both have the virtue of knowledge, would I have the same blessing?"

Brittani jumped off the fence to put an arm around

Tiara. "That is not something for either of us to know right now. However, we will discover it in time, I promise. The blessing I received was this: *'The heart of the discerning acquires knowledge, for the ears of the wise seek it out.' (Proverbs 18:15 NIV)."*

Princess Tiara repeated Brittani's blessing to herself as Kegan approached with the saddled horses. Again, she noted a flirtatious smile pass between them. Tiara giggled to herself, making a mental note to share her observation with Princess Grace. She started toward her Arabian, but curiosity stopped her.

"Excuse me, Stableman Kegan, may I ask if you've ever ridden to the Kingdom of Mysterious Peaks?"

Kegan looked from Tiara to Brittani, unsure of how to answer. Out of the corner of her eye, Tiara noted Brittani nodding at Kegan, her eyes twinkling.

"Well, Princess Tiara, yes, I have." Kegan replied. "Actually, Head Servant Joseph, Sir Scott of Floyd, and I all rode there a few weeks ago. However, we had strict instructions not to ride further than the crest of the peaks, so we were not able to see much. Why do you ask?"

"I am very curious about the plant and animal life high in those mountains. Did you see any unique animals there? Oh, and were you able to see the headwaters for Singing Creek by chance?"

Stroking the mane of Tiara's Arabian, Kegan answered, "We did not see any animals up close, though we caught sight of a leopard walking down a distant slope to a beautiful lake. We've never had a leopard in the Kingdom of Fruitful. They might be unique to the habitat of the Kingdom of Mysterious Peaks."

Tiara sensed Kegan was not revealing everything, yet she continued to give him her full attention.

Kegan continued, "Regarding the headwaters for Singing Creek, it is possible that the valley lake below the summit could be the source, although the landscape is rocky. If we are ever commissioned to return and I'm able to ride down to the lake, I'll try to determine where Singing Creek begins."

Tiara nodded, gazing up at the distant peaks.

"Thank you, Kegan," Princess Brittani interjected. "Please do keep us informed, as we are both eager to know more about that kingdom. Now, Tiara, you and I have an appointment at the Cave of Stones."

As she mounted her bay-colored Arabian, Tiara thanked Stableman Kegan. She piled her hair under her riding cap and grabbed the reins. Teasing her sister she challenged, "Brittani, I guess if knowledge can't be hurried, we'd better just saunter, right?"

With a wink, Princess Brittani retorted, "Nah, let's gallop! I bet I can beat you there!"

The two princesses galloped up the path toward the protected Cave of Stones. Neither of them noticed that while they had been talking, the Old One rode ahead on her grey Paso Fino.

CHAPTER 7

SAPPHIRE

As she laid her head on her pillow that night, Tiara smiled in anticipation of spending the next day with Prince Joshua. *Everyone in the kingdom loves Prince Joshua*, she thought, closing her eyes. *We will have to spend the day away from the villages or I'll never get a chance to even talk to him. I wonder where we'll go.* Try as she might, the excitement of spending time with the prince kept her awake. She rehearsed their conversation topics, wondering how she might explain her latest discoveries. Eventually she drifted into sleep and dreamt of the streams of color she saw in the walls of the Cave of Stones with Princess Brittani.

On the days he left the castle to walk or ride through villages, people would often follow along behind Prince Joshua. Enamored by his regal manner, they could not resist shadowing him. Because of his light auburn hair and muscular build, the young ladies of the kingdom often made their presence visible whenever he rode by.

Blessed with many talents, Joshua was a strong athlete, a remarkable musician, and had a delightful sense of humor. People loved being in his company. If he wasn't telling funny stories, he was playing guitar, singing, or participating in some type of sports. The two youngest princesses, Tiara and Grace often amused themselves by tagging behind Joshua as he walked along kingdom roads. They would giggle at the young ladies fawning over him. When athletic games took place, they'd sit on grassy fields to cheer on Joshua's team. If they knew he was singing somewhere, they'd scramble to get front row seats.

Tiara squealed the minute she heard his knock on her door. Already dressed in her favorite blue tunic, she swung open the door and began giggling nervously in excitement.

"Whoa!" Joshua cried, when he saw Tiara's messy bed covers. "It looks like you had a party with all your friends last night, little girl. What went on in here?"

This teasing caused her to laugh even harder, for she loved his attention. Joshua reached down to grab the top blanket, which had fallen on the floor near the bed. He threw it across the room, purposefully missing the bed. It landed on top of Oscar's cage.

"Hey," Tiara scolded, "Don't scare Oscar!" She proceeded to throw her pillow at Joshua, hitting him in the stomach. Their rambunctious activity went on until Tiara grew tired of laughing.

"What are we going to do today, silly prince?" she breathlessly inquired, giving Oscar some hay.

"Well, little girl," Joshua replied, "why don't you first tell me where you went yesterday with Princess Brittani."

"Oh, yes! Guess what? We were able to go inside the Cave of Stones. Father gave permission."

"Wow! That's awesome, sis! How was it? Did you see the flash of brilliant color you spoke of at dinner last week?"

"Well, we were not allowed to explore the entire cave, only to go inside the entrance to look around. I didn't see a noticeable flash, but there was an almost eerie illumination coming from deep inside. I desperately wanted to run away from the sentries to explore the light source. Then I heard Princess Desiree's voice in my head saying I must always do what's right."

Laughing, Joshua nodded. Tiara continued, "I also noticed some fascinating strains of color running throughout the walls of the cave. They were like a rainbow of sand. You see, minerals in rock can be quite colorful."

"I did not know that. I have seen rocks cracked open, though. Sometimes you can find sparkling minerals inside a broken rock."

"Yes, that's similar to what we saw. It's called crystallization." Tiara excitedly explained more, "Magma cools differently depending on conditions. When it cools very slowly, it will form crystals. That is probably what happened in the walls of the cave."

"Wow, little girl! You are always teaching me something about nature. Do you think there might be more streams of color deeper inside the Cave of Stones?"

"I wouldn't be surprised." Tiara sat down on the bed to ponder. Soon, her eyes grew big with wonder. "You could be on to something, Joshua. What if there are valuable crystallized gems deep inside the Cave of Stones? When some minerals cool, they form rubies, emeralds or even diamonds! And I'm sure there is a light source from above, like a window in the roof of the cave, causing the jewels to radiate! Oh, how I want to return to explore more."

Prince Joshua sat down next to her. "I wonder if that is why guards are stationed at the entrance of the cave. Maybe there *are* precious gems inside. Perhaps we can talk with Father about your speculation."

"Yes, let's try to find out more. I'm sure Princess Brittani will want to be in on the conversation too."

After a moment of silent thought, Joshua stood, extending his arm to Tiara to escort her down the hall, "For now, we have a different exploration journey to take. Besides, I'm walking beside the most precious jewel of all—my little sister, Princess Tiara!" He tousled her hair.

Tiara blushed, lowering her head in embarrassment. She nervously twisted a strand of hair.

"Tiara?" Joshua asked knowingly, "Are you self-conscious because I gave you a compliment?

She turned her head away, then spoke quietly, "Yes, I guess. It's silly, isn't it?"

"Not at all. Feeling uncomfortable when people admire you is a sign of humility." As they stood at the top of the stairs, Joshua took his crown out of his leather satchel and unwrapped the protective cover. He pointed to the sapphire in the center. "Believe it or not, this jewel stands for the *virtue of humility*."

Tiara implored, "Oh, please do tell me how you earned that sapphire, Prince Joshua. I am eager to hear your story."

"Of course! I will tell you the story as we walk. I'd

like to head toward the bluffs today if that's okay with you."

Tiara laced her arm through his, and they attempted to walk down the stairs like a dignified prince and princess. Joshua stopped to talk with Head Servant Joseph for a few minutes. Tiara grew impatient and tugged gently on Joshua's brown surcoat. He tousled her hair in response. Tiara tugged harder until Joseph stepped to open the castle door for the eager princess.

Once outside the castle gates, Tiara shoved Joshua to the side. "I'll race you to the Village of the Pines," she challenged.

"You're on!"

After running with abandon for several minutes, they were nearing the Village of the Pines. Tiara stopped abruptly.

"Joshua, why don't we walk along the footpath from here. If we go into the village, we will never be able to talk, just the two of us."

"Ah, yes. You are right. We need time to talk, just the two of us."

"Yes," Tiara smiled, "It's just you and me today. No lovely ladies trying to impress you are allowed to spoil our time together."

Joshua threw his head back in laughter. "Right. I

don't think I want anyone to overhear what I tell you today, anyway."

Tiara stopped and tilted her head, "Why not?"

"Well, it's rather uncomfortable for me to talk about myself so much. It feels a bit like bragging, and that causes me to feel awkward."

Tiara began walking again, "But that is what Father has proclaimed must happen, so you have an excuse to brag away. I'm eager to hear how you earned that luscious, dark sapphire, so let's get started."

They settled into a brisk stride as Prince Joshua explained how he earned the sapphire. Keenly aware that villagers liked to follow him around, he told Tiara their admiration caused him to feel uncomfortable. He admitted to sometimes taking the footpaths when he visited friends so people wouldn't notice him.

"I guess I did not realize people following you made you nervous. Perhaps Grace and I shouldn't follow you around anymore."

Joshua laughed. "I've grown used to it, but it hasn't always been easy."

Kicking a rock as he walked, he proceeded to tell of a challenging time when this admiration became a fixation. Because of their high regard for him, villagers decided to erect a statue in his honor. Sir Scott of Floyd, a good friend to Joshua, informed him of the plan. Immediately, Joshua tried to talk the villagers out of the idea, but no one listened to his pleas.

Soon after the monument was complete, Prince Joshua was riding through the kingdom when he noticed people kneeling at the statue's base. He rode in closer and realized they were praying to it. Joshua was dismayed. He knew he had to do something. That night, while everyone slept, the prince grabbed his chisel and rode to the monument. He proceeded to chisel out the entire face of the statue. He asked Sir Scott to summon the messengers, directing them to spread the word throughout the kingdom to meet at the base of the sculpture at noon the next day. It was there he gave the following speech,

"*Good people of the Kingdom of Fruitful, it is not right to worship any human being. Every person possesses wonderful talents. Why should there be a statue built in my honor? I will not allow you to pray to me. I am a young man like any other.*

"*Therefore, you can see that I have chiseled out the face of the statue. It will no longer exalt one man over others. This faceless memorial now stands in honor of every individual in the kingdom.*

"*What's more, I have convinced the king and queen to build an outdoor chapel next to this monument here on the high bluff. The chapel will remind us to worship*

*only the One True God who created us, blessing us with
the wonderful Kingdom of Fruitful."*

Prince Joshua's speech changed people's attitudes,
and they realized they were wrong to admire him that
intensely. Because of his self-effacing act, he received
his crown with the beautiful sapphire in the center,
representing the *virtue of humility*.

"Ah," Tiara responded knowingly as she kicked
away the stone Joshua played with. "Now I realize why
we are walking to the bluffs. We are going to visit the
Chapel on the Bluffs as well as the faceless statue! I've
always wondered why the memorial had no face. I
never knew it was your face that was once there." They
walked quietly for a while as Tiara pondered what the
prince had done.

"That was a very selfless thing to do," she told him.
"Why didn't you just let the people admire you? You
are a prince, you *are* incredibly talented, and your
abilities *do* shine above those of others. Besides, princes
have statues built in their honor all the time," Tiara
reminded him.

"Little girl," Joshua explained, "exalting one person
over another is the first step down a very dangerous
path. Every individual has unique abilities. Take your
knowledge of nature, for example. Your understanding
of animals and geology is tremendous, but I'm not

going to worship you because you know more than I do. What I will do is to come to you with questions about God's created world. You see, it is important to appreciate everyone's unique personality."

Tiara marveled at Joshua's humility. She now understood why the people of the kingdom called him *the humble prince*.

They reached the Chapel on the Bluffs and stood near the faceless statue. Secretly, Tiara longed for a statue built in her honor. She imagined the rock carved to show her long, chestnut hair blowing in the wind. She imagined a curvier body, like her older sisters. She pictured a paisley corset bodice with puffed sleeves, complemented by a long flowing skirt.

Prince Joshua interrupted her daydream. "What are you deep in thought about, sis?"

"Oh...uh...nothing really." Tiara shifted her position and looked away quickly. "I was just wondering about this monument. It is exceedingly difficult for princes and princesses to remain humble, don't you agree? People look to us as examples. They want to be like us. We are required to wear crowns in public. That asks for admiration, doesn't it? How can we not be proud?"

Joshua sat on the bench in front of the chapel, "There is a significant difference between pride and honor, little sister. I agree that wearing a crown has the potential to inflate one's ego. However, our highly esteemed roles give us responsibility as well as opportunity. Try to look at it this way: with honor comes the privilege of serving. Helping people in need, interacting with villagers, setting up systems for learning like Princess Brittani, or being an ambassador to neighboring kingdoms, like Princess Desiree—these were all opportunities for service. Even overseeing a project like building this chapel was a profound opportunity because it blesses people with an actual place to worship God."

Joshua's words caused Tiara to regret daydreaming about a statue built as tribute to her. She sat beside her brother and leaned forward, thinking. She realized the importance of laying down any pride associated with being a princess. However, she was quite sure the gem she would earn for her own crown would *not* be a sapphire. She had much to learn about being humble.

Needing to adjust her line of thinking, Tiara turned to face Joshua. "I think you are supposed to tell me about your crowning ceremony, right? You know, about the blessing from that mysterious *Book of Truth*?"

"Oh, I didn't realize you knew about the *Book of Truth*. Well, I'm happy to share more. The blessing the

Old One...uh..." Joshua stopped himself from saying too much. "I mean the blessing from the old *Book of Truth* for me was this: '*When pride comes, then comes disgrace, but with the humble is wisdom*' *(Proverbs 11:2 ESV)*."

Prince Joshua hung his head thinking about his mistake. Tiara was not ready to know about the old woman yet. *Yikes, I almost blew it.* Looking over at Tiara, he noticed she was deep in thought. Before she had a chance to consider his mention of the Old One, Joshua quickly changed the subject.

"Would you like to go over to the stables with me? I promised to play polo with Sir Scott of Floyd and Kegan the Stableman."

It was the perfect distraction. A broad smile spread over Tiara's face. "You know what? I think Kegan and Princess Brittani may have a fondness for each other. Yesterday, when we went riding, they were smiling at each other quite flirtatiously."

"Ha! Could be," Prince Joshua said, being careful not to speculate. "Shall we go?"

Princess Tiara hesitated, glancing at the doors to the Chapel on the Bluffs. "Can I meet you there in a few minutes? I think I would like to go into the chapel to pray, since we're here. Is that okay?"

"Absolutely. Praying is the wisest, most humble

step anyone can take. I will never stand in the way of anyone who wants to pray, as long as they pray ONLY to God."

Joshua pulled Tiara in for a hug, then tousled her hair again. "See you in a while, little girl. Take time to pray. It will not be wasted." Then the prince jogged off toward the stables.

She watched her brother disappear into the distance. Surprised by her own maturity, Princess Tiara approached the chapel doors made of simple white pine from the nearby village. She traced her fingers over the carving of flowers delicately adorning the façade of the doors. She breathed deeply before entering the place of worship.

Beams of light shone from the stained-glass windows lining the walls of the simple chapel. Images from her beloved forest prominently centered each window. The lovely nature scenes warmed her heart. *I should come here more often,* she told herself as she walked down the center aisle. Her hands grazed over the tops of the cherry wood benches until she came to the mahogany kneeling bench at the altar.

She knelt.

I am learning a lot, she prayed. *But I still have no idea of my virtue. I ask for wisdom in the days ahead as I face whatever challenge comes. Let me not be afraid.*

Sometimes, I just yearn to run away to the Meadow of Hyacinths. Or I want to ignore the rules and sneak off to explore the Cave of Stones. I don't want to make any mistakes. I'd like to be as righteous as Princess Desiree or as knowledgeable as Princess Brittani or as humble as Prince Joshua. Help me make the right decisions, Lord. Amen.

With her eyes closed in prayer, Princess Tiara did not see an old woman sitting on a pew in the back of the chapel. Nor did she notice the radiant glow of color that filled the small sanctuary as she prayed. By the time she opened her eyes and rose to leave, the Old One had already disappeared, the glow vanishing with her.

CHAPTER 8

GARNET

At dinner the night before, Princess Lauren told Tiara they would be riding to the Village of Eagles for their time together. Knowing it would be a full day, Tiara woke up early to dress in her riding clothes. *I wonder why we are journeying so far away. I know Princess Lauren rides to a different village each week, but why would she choose the one farthest from the castle?* Tiara laid her breeches and surcoat on the bed before making sure Oscar had enough food and water.

"It will be a long time before I return," she spoke to Oscar. "I suspect Sir Scott of Floyd will accompany us. I know Father requires him to ride with Lauren for protection."

She arranged hay and raw vegetables in Oscar's cage. "I'd better take my quill pen and parchments so we can write down what we observe. Lauren always reports to Father after visiting the townspeople." She added the pen and parchment to her satchel.

In anticipation, Tiara opened the door to look for her sister, who startled her by being right at the chamber door. Initially, she flinched at the surprise, but then relaxed with a laugh. "Oh, you're here, Princess Lauren. I'm ready to go."

Graceful beauty stood before her, and Tiara slowed her excitement to gaze admiringly at her sister. Normally, Lauren wore her light brown hair straight down her back, but today she pulled it up in a bun stuck under her brown velvet riding hat. Wearing dark green breeches and a beige chemisette, Lauren never dressed pretentiously. Though she carried her crown in a satchel, she did not wear it. Her ivory skin and marble grey eyes glistened as a gentle smile spread over her face. Tiara lost herself looking at Lauren's mysterious eyes. The silvery flecks of color created an ambience of light in shadow. Tiara often thought Lauren's eyes almost matched Oscar's fur.

Lauren's voice brought Tiara out of her trance, "Good morning, sweet sister. I see you are ready. It's difficult to wake up so early, isn't it?" Princess Lauren gently brushed a loose strand of Tiara's hair away from her face. "Tell me how you're feeling about today's journey to the Village of Eagles."

Tiara adjusted her paddock boots, "Well, I guess I am a little nervous. It is a long ride, and I have heard that the people in the village are not entirely happy with Father these days. Honestly, Lauren, I am not sure what to expect."

Lauren smiled and nodded. She grabbed Tiara's satchel in one hand and took Tiara's hand with the other. "Let's go down to the vestibule and talk about what to anticipate, though we also may be surprised with interactions we can't yet imagine."

They sat on the brocade upholstered bench near the turret with the largest window. It was Lauren's favorite reading spot. Once comfortable, Lauren explained the plan, "I am going to take you to the place I discovered a particularly important truth. It will not be an easy visit, you are right. You will meet an interesting person, perhaps many precious souls."

"Is this the village where you earned the lovely red garnet in your crown? Can you tell me about it before we go?"

"Of course." Sensing Tiara's angst, Lauren took the crown out of the bag and laid it near the window, pointing to the jewel in the center. "This red garnet stands for the *virtue of compassion*. I earned it on a day that changed my life forever."

Five years ago, Lauren rode along the roads of the Village of Eagles in the easternmost part of the kingdom where many poorer families lived. Lauren heard about the town from Princess Desiree and decided she wanted to determine what she could do to help.

"At the top of a hill leading to the village, I stopped to study what lay ahead. Suddenly, an older, disheveled man jumped out from the bushes. He ran right in front of Biscuit and me, completely blocking the way. I immediately pulled Biscuit's reins to a stop. The man needed food, and because he recognized me, he demanded I give him some."

Tiara straightened and leaned toward Lauren, "Oh my gosh! You must have been terrified. I am guessing Sir Scott of Floyd apprehended this man right away."

"Actually no, for this was before Father assigned Sir Scott to ride with me. I rode alone."

"Princess Lauren, if this was five years ago, you were only twelve, my age. You must have been terrified! What did you do?"

"At first, I was scared, then I found myself angered by the fact the man was so demanding. Mostly, I was confused. A part of me wanted to ride back home as fast as I could but something stopped me. Instead, I dismounted and looked the man straight in the eye. I must admit I prayed for help throughout the encounter. Soon, I had an idea."

"I'm feeling nervous for you, Princess Lauren. Please tell me about your idea." Tiara scooted closer.

Lauren asked the man to take her into the village. At first, he refused, but once she convinced him she would secure food for him, the man agreed. When they arrived, Lauren observed the people in the village turning their backs to the man. It was obvious they wanted nothing to do with him. Noticing how he hung his head in shame, Lauren's heart of compassion stirred. She decided she must do something to help. She went to a local shopkeeper and purchased bread, fresh vegetables, and ham. The princess then walked with the man to the center of town where the well was. She drew water, motioning for him to sit down under a shady tree.

"I left him at the well and went to speak with several proprietors regarding why they avoided the man. I discovered that he begged for food daily, yet never did any work for the village. The hardworking townspeople perceived him to be a nuisance, not worthy of their alms."

Once she understood the circumstances, Lauren

asked several shopkeepers if they would agree to give the man food in exchange for his doing odd jobs. Though some hesitated, several agreed, for all had chores needing to be done. Lauren arranged for the man to do specific tasks for the shopkeepers. She planned for him to receive food, a place to sleep, and a small monetary stipend as long as he did his share of the work.

"When I explained the plan to the poor man, he began to cry. He told me he had wandered the kingdom alone for years. No one had ever made time to help him before. It took me all afternoon to arrange things, however I did not mind. In the end, a person in need would enjoy a more fulfilling life than ever before."

Tiara shook her head and sat back against the stone wall of the turret. "I am amazed you did all this for someone you did not know. For someone who even threatened you. He did not really want to help himself. You could have just given him food and moved on. Why did you spend half a day trying to help?"

"I understand why one might think it would be enough to just give him food and water. His *threats*, as you say, came from desperation," Lauren explained as she stood and moved to the window, waiting. Tiara sensed there was more to say, so she joined her sister at the window. Tiara noticed a faraway look in Lauren's silvery grey eyes. "Showing true compassion often means taking the time to solve a problem. We must never ignore someone, no matter how demanding they are, because there is always a need behind their anger."

Lauren breathed in and turned to face Tiara, "If I simply gave him food, he would have found himself in the same situation the very next day. To earn his own provision was his true need."

Looking out the window herself, Tiara understood why people referred to Lauren as *the compassionate princess*. Compassion was more than just giving to people in need. It involved helping them solve problems, finding a path for future success. That took time and effort.

Tiara pondered Lauren's challenge further. "I understand why Father assigned Sir Scott of Floyd to accompany you when you go visiting. He is there just in case someone's pleading gets dangerous."

Lauren nodded, "Yes, even though the events of that day led me to receive this garnet in my crown, Father did insist I never again ride unaccompanied."

"Okay, now comes the part where you tell me about your blessing from the *Book of Truth*. Yes, I know about the *Book of Truth*. My whole family has been acting mysteriously lately, yet I am finding ways to figure out what you all are up to."

Lauren laughed, "Good for you, sister." She took Tiara's hand and walked toward the castle entrance. "The blessing I received makes me smile every time I rehearse it in my mind. *'Greater love has no one than this: to lay down one's life for one's friends' (John 15:13 NIV)."*

Giving Tiara time to process the power of the verse, Lauren grew quiet for a few minutes. Just as they reached the castle entrance where Head Servant Joseph waited, she stopped and spoke again, "My dear sister, there is a reason we are taking time to prepare you for your crowning ceremony. If you're wise, you must realize this."

Tiara pursed her lips and looked up as if studying the ceiling. "I suppose I need to see this ceremony as a valuable time in life. Though I hate to admit it, I think it is part of growing up. I imagine all of you probably had the same doubts and curiosities I have right now."

"Indeed, we did. Yes, it is part of maturing. You mustn't resent it. Once you receive your crown and gem, your heart transforms in many ways."

Lauren glanced at Head Servant Joseph, who bowed his head. She smiled pensively, "You like to explore, right? Try to think of the months ahead as a new part of life to discover. It may not contain the actual beauty of God's creation that you see, smell, and physically experience when you're roaming the kingdom. However, it holds different mysteries just as important. Does that make sense?"

Tiara nodded in agreement, looking down with crinkled brow as she wondered about her future. She knew Lauren's words were important. Still, she was not sure she was ready to grow up. It felt like it was coming too fast.

With resolve, Tiara raised her head and resumed walking, "I am guessing we will ride to the easternmost part of the kingdom today. We have not even left the castle yet. We'd better get going."

"Yes, sister," Lauren smiled a smile that would melt the hardest of hearts, her silvery grey eyes looking at Tiara as if they could see into her soul. "We'll visit that same man to find out if he's working hard for the good of the village. We'll also look for others we might help."

Suddenly, Tiara bounced in excitement with an idea, "Before we go, I need to get something." She grabbed her satchel and ran to the pantry. Lauren could barely keep up as Tiara disappeared through the kitchen. She soon saw Tiara loading her satchel with food. With a knowing smile, Lauren turned to leave the kitchen area. At the other end of the room, she caught sight of an old woman in a colorful cape who promptly nodded, returning Lauren's smile.

Throughout their time in Eagle Village, Tiara observed her older sister. She noted Lauren's genuine smile as she interacted. Lauren's quiet gentleness was so different than Brittani's bubbly enthusiasm or Desiree's strength of principle. Tiara realized immediately that compassion required humility, like Joshua's virtue. Yet, with Lauren, there was also intentional action. It was as if Princess Lauren could not restrain the love that flowed from her heart. Tiara marveled at how her more reserved sister seemed energized by connecting with people.

The villagers' needs were plenty. Many complained, with some presenting a list of what they wanted. With each grievance, Lauren spent time to help figure out how the need could be satisfied. It was a day of problem-solving as much as a day of showing kindness. Once they mounted their steeds, Tiara was exhausted.

Sir Scott of Floyd rode quietly behind the two princesses as the sun began to lower on their return home. Tiara wondered what it would be like to have a soldier riding with you all the time. It did make her feel safe, yet it also caused her to focus more intently on duty. She was not certain she liked the idea of being responsible.

During the long ride, Tiara began to daydream about the freedom of the forest. She saw herself standing on top of a huge boulder gazing at the hills across Singing Creek. How she longed to simply sit with Socky, listening to him purr as he rubbed against her leg. Then she remembered the day with Princess Desiree. Together they ran through the forest, and it was fun. The days with Brittani and Joshua were also enjoyable. In the past four days, she had given more thought to deeper ideas of life than ever before. There had to be a way to show the virtue of a dignified princess and still have a bit of freedom's fun, too. She could only hope.

CHAPTER 9

EMERALD

It was dark by the time the two sisters returned to the castle. Princess Tiara changed into her sleeping gown the minute she entered her bed chamber. She let Oscar run around the room since he'd been in his cage nearly the entire day. As she watched him scurry to his favorite places, she continued processing thoughts about the time at Eagle Village. The demands and needs of the people in the easternmost part of the kingdom disturbed her. While she learned a lot about compassion, she worried what her own virtue might demand.

Once Oscar was safely back in his cage, Tiara crawled into bed, hoping for a good night's sleep. But her thoughts continued to keep her awake. *I know I'm supposed to have a special virtue like my brothers and sisters. I just don't know what it is. I will never be as compassionate as Princess Lauren. That is too exhausting! I don't have much humility in me like Prince Joshua. I dream too much about being admired. It's clear I struggle to always make the right choice like Princess Desiree. Too often, I make mistakes with my decisions. Also, while I know a lot about nature and animals, I still have much to learn. I can't imagine being as intelligent as Princess Brittani. What virtue will I have? How will I earn the jewel for my crown?*

Sleep finally came, but with it a fitful dream. Hundreds of gems circled around her head. She reached to grab each jewel, yet no matter how hard she tried, she was unable to grasp one. She found herself anxiously running over the bridge to Forest Valley following these circling gems. She chased them to the Cave of Stones, stopping at the entrance. She ran to the stables to ask Kegan to saddle up her Arabian, thinking she could move faster with the speed of a horse. Still, she was unsuccessful in capturing the elusive jewels. She tossed and turned until the dream took her to the Chapel on the Bluffs. There, she knelt in prayer. The dream didn't allow her to know the words she uttered, but restful sleep eventually blanketed the young princess. While she slept, Tiara was oblivious to the old woman sitting next to her bedside whispering, "There, there, Princess Tiara. Everything is going to be all right."

Princess Grace knocked for the third time, then hesitantly opened the door to Tiara's chamber. Seeing her younger sister still in bed, Grace sat down on the bed and whispered, "Are you awake, Tiara? Are you ready for our day together?"

Tiara stirred and opened one eye. A brief, pursed smile immediately transformed to a frown. Princess Grace laid her hand on Tiara's shoulder, "What's the matter, sis?"

Slowly raising herself to a seated position, Tiara recounted her dream to Grace. She spilled out her worries. "I just don't think I have a virtue that fits me. Before, I never cared about a gem in my crown. Now, it is all I think about. What if I never earn my jewel?" Tiara held her head in her hands as tears flowed.

"I see," Grace responded, scooting closer. "I understand your concern. This is a momentous time in life for you, isn't it?"

Tiara sniffed. "I just don't want to think about it anymore."

Grace hugged her in silence, gently giving her sister a kerchief.

At length, Grace spoke, "Listen to me, Little 'T'. You are full of goodness and will easily prove yourself to be virtuous. I do not know any other person in this kingdom who cares as much for animals as you do. That takes virtue. I also know how devoted you are to the joy of discovery. In all your explorations, you are curious as well as patient."

Grace paused briefly waiting for Tiara's emotions to subside. "There is a reason Mother and Father are having you spend these days with us. We know you cannot figure this out on your own. You are not meant to. We are here to help you. Trust me, you *do* have a virtue. You *will* earn a jewel for your crown. You don't have to do it alone, though."

Princess Grace grabbed Tiara's hands and stood, helping her sister up. "Like a rope braided with many strands, we will all come together to help you be strong through this process of discovery. You've waited many years to find out what gem you will wear in your crown, surely you can wait a little longer?"

Grace's encouraging words were just what Tiara needed to hear. The reassurance eased her worries. "Thank you. I feel better." She straightened her sleeping gown and tried to rearrange her messy hair.

Then, as if a cloud lifted, she grabbed her sister's hands. "Okay, Princess Grace, how will we spend our time together today?"

Aware of Tiara's mood change, Grace began to speak but stopped when out of the corner of her eye she saw the curtains across the room move slightly. Glimpsing the edge of a colorful cloak, Grace immediately knew it was the mysterious, old woman, so she squinted and focused as unobtrusively as she could. The Old One held a bouquet of flowers from the Meadow of Hyacinths. Grace needed to rethink the plans for the day.

"Um, why don't we go pick flowers in the Meadow of Hyacinths today?" Gracie suggested.

"Are you serious?" Tiara was thrilled. "It is mid-spring. I was there with both Desiree and Brittani earlier this week. It was full of blooms ready to pop. Today there should be tons of flowers to pick."

"Sounds like fun!" Grace replied. Closer in age to each other, Princess Grace and Tiara were friends as well as sisters. Climbing the hills near Forest Valley was one of their favorite activities. Often their days included lengthy discussions about nothing and everything.

Grace knew Tiara needed to just have fun. *She is only twelve years old, after all,* Grace thought. *Still, I must find a way to tell her how I earned my emerald.* The jewel in Grace's crown was a luscious, green emerald, which provided a lovely contrast to the loose curls of her shoulder-length copper hair. It was important to respect what Tiara needed, and not give her more to worry about. This was what the Old One silently communicated earlier. Because of that, Grace decided she would not talk about her crown or jewel unless Tiara brought it up.

Once Tiara was dressed, the sisters bounded down the stairs, waving a hurried good-bye to Head Servant Joseph, who smiled broadly as he watched them scamper across castle grounds. Instead of stopping to open the stone fence gate, they challenged each other to hurdle the two-foot-tall structure, creating a shortcut. Joseph laughed and shook his head at their antics. He knew young princesses needed to act like normal girls occasionally.

They soon arrived at the Meadow of Hyacinths. Once they saw the vibrant colors of pink peonies, orange poppies and purple hyacinths, they plopped down in the grass. Each picked an armful of flowers, then strolled to the wooden bridge over Singing Creek.

"This is such an amazing meadow. We should come here more often."

"Yes, it is," Tiara responded. "I love all the bright

colors, and the lush, green leaves. Hey! The leaves are almost the same color as the emerald in your crown!"

Grace took off the crown and looked at the gem, trying to decide if this was her opportunity to explain her virtue.

Tiara did not give her a chance, "Tell me how you earned your beautiful emerald, Grace. I want to listen to your story. I'm surprised I don't already know it since we always talk."

Smiling in relief, Grace began, "You might know part of my story. Let's see what you remember. The emerald stands for the *virtue of loyalty*. You know, how to stick by your friends and family in all kinds of situations, even difficult ones."

"Oh, I totally understand!" Tiara shook her head in vigorous agreement. "You are a loyal sister. Whoever decided on your virtue picked the right one! I'm eager to hear what blessing from the *Book of Truth* you received, too."

"Well, thank you!" Grace laid her crown on the bridge and arranged her bouquet inside. Then she raised herself to sit on the bridge's rail. "I will start there and then recount the events of my story. The blessing I received on crowning day was this: *'Don't let love and truth ever leave you. Tie them around your neck. Write them on the tablet of your heart' (Proverbs 3:3, NIRV).*

"You see, loyalty is a combination of devotion and encouragement. You know how we love to talk about silly things? And every so often, we discuss our feelings and worries, too, right? Well, when you are a loyal friend, you must always be ready to speak words of support when someone is discouraged or concerned."

This made perfect sense. Tiara was thankful to hear about a virtue that seemed easier to define. Readying herself for the story, she climbed on top of the opposite rail of the bridge facing Grace.

Grace continued, "In all honesty, the way I earned this emerald makes me sad. You see, I have always tried to be kind to everyone in my group of friends. Sadly, not all my friends at school were nice to each other. Do you remember Rosemary?"

Tiara nodded.

"Well, a few years ago, Rosemary was singled out by Elizabeth, Diana, and Anne. They simply decided they no longer wanted to be friends with her."

"That's horrible!" Tiara's eyes flashed.

"It gets worse. They started accusing her of things she'd never done. Even some of the teachers at school believed their lies. For whatever reason, they decided to basically banish Rosemary from our group of friends."

"What did you do?"

Grace shook her head. "I was baffled because I could see no reason for their scheme. Rosemary is one of the sweetest girls I know. I tried to talk them out of such harassment, although they insisted. Because I could not support the mistreatment, I chose to remain loyal to Rosemary." She lowered her head with a soft cry, "That choice meant I lost the friendship of all the other girls. It still upsets me. I had to make the faithful choice. Though I wanted to be loyal to all of them, I chose Rosemary and let everyone else be responsible for their own decisions."

With tears welling up, Tiara spoke her support, "Grace, I am proud of you for sticking by her. You were truly faithful. I'm sure Rosemary felt horribly rejected."

"Yes." Grace gathered composure before continuing. "This is where words of encouragement come in. She needed assurance that such cruelty was undeserved. I wrote many letters of support and spent time just listening to her. It was difficult to see her hurt. And it made me sad to lose those other friendships," Grace said wistfully.

"That makes sense," Tiara replied thoughtfully. "You could only prove your own loyalty, and you could not control the behavior of others. Did you ever become friends with Elizabeth, Diana, and Anne again?"

"Not completely, though we are all cordial to each other now. I think over time, they realized how cruel they'd been. I don't think I'll ever understand why they targeted Rosemary. Sometimes meanness rears its ugly head for no reason, I guess."

Tiara pondered Grace's struggle, realizing that loyalty is not as easy as it seems. Wanting to encourage, she said, "You are also a very loyal sister to me. I was upset this morning, but you reassured me. I really appreciate it."

Grace smiled. The sisters sat in silence for a while. Then, almost in unison, both girls jumped down off the bridge railing. As they resumed picking flowers, Tiara told Grace about Stableman Kegan smiling at Princess Brittani. She mimicked Brittani smiling back. She also told her about praying in the Chapel on the Bluffs. They decided they'd visit the chapel together in the coming days.

As the two princesses meandered back to the castle, there was an uncharacteristic silence. Tiara considered the unique value of each of her sibling's virtues. As she reflected on the virtue of loyalty, she was keenly aware of how close it was to devotion.

CHAPTER 10

TOPAZ

E ven though he was her brother, Prince Burton, or B.K., puzzled Tiara. At times she wondered if he knew she was in the room. Then like a shifting shadow, he would sit forward, squint, and pay close attention. Unsure how to figure him out, Tiara hoped spending the day with her brother would shed light on his unique mannerisms.

She woke up excited as well as nervous. At fourteen, B.K. was closest in age to Tiara. A tall, quiet-mannered young man with sandy brown, cropped hair, Prince B.K. was contemplative. Though he dutifully attended royal events with the rest of the family, he preferred to be alone with his thoughts.

"I wonder what we'll talk about," Tiara whispered to Oscar. "I know the jewel in B.K.'s crown is a gold topaz, but I do not know what virtue it represents. Since he does not talk much, maybe it's the virtue of silence?" She giggled.

Tiara tidied up her bedchamber to pass the time. When the clock struck 9:00 a.m., she wondered if he'd forgotten. She quickly swung the door open upon hearing a knock. It was *not* Prince Burton on the other side, however, but a messenger delivering a note. *This must be a brand-new messenger*, Tiara reasoned, for she was not dressed in the typical uniform. Opening the parchment, Tiara read the note aloud to Oscar:

> *Dear Princess Tiara, I am climbing the rocks on the far side of Singing Creek. Please dress comfortably and join me. Prince B.K.*

"I should have known," Tiara confided. "I often see B.K. climbing those rocks. Once he told me they help him think. Well, I guess I can find my way there with no problem." Placing Oscar back in his cage, she grabbed her satchel and left her bedchambers. After a few steps, Tiara stopped and looked back, suddenly realizing the recently hired servant looked vaguely familiar, though she could not place her. By this time, the new steward had already descended the stairs with her face out of view. Tiara briefly wondered why the messenger was not wearing the typical gold tunic and white apron female servants were required to wear. Shrugging her shoulders, the princess hurried down the stairs, intending to ask Princess Desiree what she knew about the new servant.

"Prince B.K., I'm here," Tiara yelled upon arriving at the rock outcropping near Singing Creek. "Where are you?"

She felt a gentle tapping on her shoulder and twirled around to see B.K. "Oh, you startled me. I thought you were up on those rocks somewhere."

Prince B.K. smiled, waving his hand in the direction of the road to Cornucopia Village. "Let's go this way," he said quietly.

"I thought we were going to climb rocks?" Tiara asked.

"Oh, I was just climbing them this morning to think about what to say today." B.K. started walking, and Tiara hurried to follow. They strolled in silence for a while.

"How have you spent the last days with our siblings?" B.K. asked, trying to make conversation. Tiara explained in detail what she learned from their siblings. She could not tell if B.K. was listening because he kept looking up at the hills or glancing further down the road as if he were searching for something.

After Tiara finished recounting her previous five days, B.K. asked, "Do you know what *your* virtue is, yet?"

"Not at all. It is starting to frustrate me, to be honest. I have no idea how to prove myself to be a virtuous princess."

B.K smiled, looking to the sky again. "Well, honesty is a good thing, however, so is patience. I think you will know more after our day together."

"Really? I hope you are right. Are you going to help me figure it all out?"

"Perhaps," B.K. replied vaguely. Tiara waited for him to say more, but he just kept walking. As they neared the village, they saw a crowd of children gathered at the town park. B.K. stopped near a large oak tree.

"Tell me, Princess Tiara, what do you see?" B.K. asked, as he pointed toward the children.

"I see children playing games in the park, of course," Tiara responded quickly. "From here, it looks like one of them is pretending to be a horse or something, because the others are jumping on top of him. I cannot tell for sure because of this big tree."

B.K. nodded, creasing his brow. He beckoned with his hand, "Come back over here a bit up on this small hill. Look again. Look very closely. Tell me what you see."

Puzzled, Tiara followed him back to the top of a small hill. She turned to observe again from the new vantage point.

"Oh no!" Tiara cried. "The children are not pretending to be riding a horse at all. That is *not* another child, it is a poor dog! They are jumping on top of that dog!" She looked at her brother for help. B.K. simply nodded, squinting, but focused on the scene.

Tiara glared at the children, and then back at B.K. Again, he stood still. Why wasn't he doing anything about this cruelty? Her brows snapped together as she placed her hands on her hips and frowned at her brother. Once more, B.K. responded with the same steady gaze. She could not bear to see the dog picked on any longer. Princess Tiara whirled around and ran down the hill.

"Stop! Please stop! You are hurting the dog," Tiara cried out. "This is not right! This animal cannot defend itself against you. Look at its tail between his legs. See the wide pupils in his eyes. He is terrified!"

Startled by the confrontation, the children stopped. One stocky boy wearing overalls whispered, "It's Princess Tiara! We'd better get out of here!" A messy-haired girl in a dirty yellow pinafore squared her shoulders and marched up to the princess.

"You think just because you are a princess, we must do what you say, huh? Well, I do not answer to anyone, Princess Tiara," she declared snidely. "Leave us alone. We don't have to do what you say. You don't even wear a crown yet."

Standing tall, Tiara replied calmly, "I am not *telling* you to stop because I am a princess. I am *asking* you to stop because what you are doing is cruel." Tiara focused her eyes fiercely on the brash girl. Prince B.K. continued to keep his distance, watching intently. Behind B.K. an old woman wrapped in a colorful cloak sat on a stone bench, also studying the scene.

One by one, the children slowly walked away. Even the ringleader backed off as she saw the others exiting the park, yet not without getting in one more accusation. "We're leaving, but not because you asked us to. We are just tired of this stupid old dog and have better things to do."

Like a sturdy post, Tiara stood immovable, her eyes scrutinizing the children as they left. Promptly, she knelt by the large, black, floppy-eared dog. "Are you okay?" she asked. "Did they hurt you?" Chained to a tree, the animal shook in fear. Tiara gently removed the chain, noting relief in the dog's deep brown eyes. She petted it tenderly, checking to be sure he was not hurt.

"There, there, little guy. You're okay now. I'm here to keep you safe." Tiara continued efforts to soothe the animal, until an idea came. "Why don't Prince B.K. and I take you with us to the castle?" she spoke quietly. "I promise to take excellent care of you."

Tiara marched back up the hill with the dog at her heels. Still upset with her brother, she refused to glance at him and marched ahead. She walked right past the Old One sitting on the bench behind the tree. B.K. paced himself to stay a few yards behind, unaffected by Tiara's anger. Eventually, her stride relaxed, and she slowed her pace.

Finally able to look him in the eye, Tiara turned around.

"Why didn't you help me, Prince Burton? You just stood there while this dog was being tortured. Just because your *assignment* was to tell me about your crown does not mean you couldn't have helped."

B.K. nodded, but that was all. Tiara tilted her head in wonder. *Why is he always so calm?* The dog ran to B.K., who knelt to scratch him behind the ears. Surprisingly, the dog rolled over in submission allowing the prince to tickle its tummy. Tiara observed

B.K.'s tenderness and realized he did care about what those mean children had done.

She cautiously joined her brother and the dog, sitting on the bare ground. "I'm sorry if I took us away from what you wanted to do today. I just could not stand by letting those kids pick on this poor dog."

Prince Burton smiled as he rubbed the dog's belly. "You did what you felt was right. You were very brave to defend this innocent animal."

She furrowed her forehead and shook her head, still unsure about her brother's mild reactions. After a few minutes, Tiara continued, "B.K., can you tell me why you knew that I should back up to observe those children from the top of the hill? How did you know I would see what was actually taking place there?"

B.K. measured his answer, "I have learned most problems can't be fully understood unless you're able to see a bigger picture of the circumstances. I thought you might see things more clearly if you looked from a different angle, getting a broader view. Does that make sense?"

"Sort of," Tiara replied. "I could not see what was really happening when I was too close and at the wrong angle, so I needed to move further away to see the entire scene more distinctly. I hope I did not embarrass you by speaking harshly to those cruel children."

"Not at all, Tiara," B.K. assured her. "As I said, you were brave. You sized up the situation first and your knowledge of dogs told you he could be badly hurt. Therefore, you intervened to make things right. Admiringly, you showed compassion, yet you never took advantage of your status as princess. Finally, you promised to be a loyal friend and care for the dog."

Tiara stopped petting and stared at her brother with her mouth wide open. Every phrase B.K. used referenced the virtues of her older brothers and sisters. She thought of Princess Desiree, always doing the right thing despite the consequences. She considered how Princess Brittani used her knowledge in many different ways. She remembered Prince Joshua's humility, not allowing his status as prince to cause pride. She reflected on Princess Lauren, showing true compassion in helping solve problems for those in need. Then she smiled to think of Princess Grace, being such a faithful friend.

"B.K., do you realize you just mentioned all the virtues of our brothers and sisters?"

"Yes," B.K. nodded. "Do you realize I included two additional virtues? Did you catch what they were?"

Tiara thought back through B.K.'s words. "Well, I

remember you saying that I had sized up the situation. Could that be a virtue?"

B.K. smiled. "Yes. That virtue just happens to be mine." He took off his crown and pointed to the gold topaz. "This topaz stands for the *virtue of perspective.*"

"Per-spek-tive? What is that?"

"Let me explain. Remember how I told you to step back to get a broader view? Well, I developed this practice a few years ago on those rocks you often see me climbing."

Tiara leaned back on her hands and listened intently as he told her about the day he walked along the far side of Singing Creek. The water flowed extra swiftly when suddenly he heard the mournful cry of one of the calves from the fields.

"I could hear, but not see, though I knew a calf was in danger. I searched around frantically to determine what I might do. I realized I was becoming too panicked, so I took a deep breath and glanced up at the outcropping of rocks near the creek. It was then I decided to climb higher in the hopes of getting a better view. Once high enough, I could see the calf caught in underbrush where the current flowed rapidly."

His next problem was to figure out how to save the calf. He stepped back further and noticed a sturdy tree branch the calf could walk on. B.K. could not lift it by himself, so he looked farther up the river where he noticed Stableman Kegan hiking. Prince B.K. yelled for help, and within minutes he and Kegan rescued the little calf.

"If I hadn't gotten some distance to gain perspective on the situation, I never would have seen where the calf was, nor would I have seen the tree branch, nor Kegan. After it happened, I realized I'd discovered a method for solving problematic situations. We need to see the bigger picture of every problem to know how to solve it. It is because of this that I am known as *the prince with perspective.*"

"*That's* why you are always climbing those rocks," Tiara surmised, sitting forward now. "You must be up there literally trying to see the bigger picture!"

Prince B.K. smiled.

Tiara urged, "Now you need to share what blessing from the *Book of Truth* you received at your crowning ceremony."

B.K. nodded, rose to a stand, and pulled a slip of parchment from his brown leather vest to read. "*To start being wise you must first get wisdom. No matter what it costs, get understanding*" (Proverbs 4:7 NIRV).

Tiara gazed at the distant hills awhile, "Perspective is sort of a combination of knowledge and wisdom, right?"

"That is a good definition, Tiara. I would add to your definition a yearning to understand every aspect of a situation."

Standing quickly, Tiara threw her hands in the air and shouted, "Oh my gosh! I think I will have the same virtue as you, B.K.! I love learning. And now I love perspective! You have really taught me a lot about how to size up a situation. Will my gem also be a gold topaz, do you know?"

Prince B.K. laughed and began walking on. "Guess I forgot to tell you that patience is also involved in the definition of perspective. Be patient, Tiara. You will have answers very soon."

Tiara furrowed her brow again, marveling at her brother's continual steady emotion. She looked around as if searching for someone else to join in with her excitement, but when she found no one, she shrugged her shoulders and caught up with the prince.

With the dog trotting between them, they headed toward the rocks at Singing Creek, ending the day climbing. Prince B.K. remained quiet and calm, making for peaceful hours on the rocks. Pleasantly content, Tiara realized she knew her brother much better now. She understood why he preferred to be alone with his thoughts, for his thoughts were very wise!

Tiara picked up Oscar to cuddle him that evening after dinner. Lowering the chinchilla, she introduced it to the dog she had rescued that afternoon. She named the canine Burton, after her brother. Her parents agreed to let her keep the new animal friend as long as he did not chew things. Of course, they made sure Head Servant Joseph also approved of the special circumstance. Surprisingly, the dog was extremely loyal and obedient. Burton (the dog) sniffed Oscar, causing the chinchilla to wince. Tiara spoke soothingly as the two animals became familiar with each other.

A bit later, Princess Tiara looked out upon the beautiful Kingdom of Fruitful from the window of her bedchamber. She knew what was coming next—her crowning. After the day with Prince B.K., she wondered again if her virtue would be the same as his, for she loved the combination of wisdom and knowledge. Of course, she would need to work on being patient. Then she began to second-guess herself. Why would two children have the same virtue? That wasn't sensible.

She thought about all the virtues of her siblings. *I guess I would be okay with any of their virtues. However, if mine is to be unique, I have no idea what it would be.*

"Oh Oscar... Oh Burton... why am I still confused?"

Oscar snuggled close against her neck and Burton lifted his wet nose under her hanging hand. With a sigh, Tiara carried Oscar back to his cage, then placed a large, overstuffed quilt she'd found for Burton's bed. She sat on the floor next to Burton, coaxing him to lay down.

"For different reasons we are both afraid, aren't we, boy? I promise you are safe here. Oscar will be a good companion, and I will spend as much time as I can with you. We can go for walks every day. I think you charmed Kitchen Steward Aurora, too. She oversees the kitchen and cooking, so I'm glad she likes you. Don't worry about your future here, Burton. You're going to love being part of our family."

Petting the dog helped them both relax. Tiara replayed her last sentences to the dog. *Don't worry about your future here, Burton. You're going to love being part of our family. Ha!* She laughed to herself. *I should take my own advice. Whatever happens at the crowning ceremony tomorrow is going to be fine. I have the most wonderful family, and I am not alone.*

CHAPTER 11

THE CROWNING

As anticipated, the king and queen summoned their children to the Great Hall the next morning. Tiara could not keep her knees from wiggling back and forth as the children formed a line outside the large, oak doors to the hall. Today would be a formal ceremony—a decisive moment—where she would be the center of attention.

Head Servant Joseph announced their arrival as the children entered and approached the elegant marble platform. As she stepped inside the large, oak doors, Tiara spotted an old woman sitting along the side of the room. She wore a multi-colored cape. Tiara recognized the woman as the new messenger who knocked on her bedroom door with a message from Prince B.K. Forgetting the expectation for silence in the presence of the king and queen, she whispered to her sister, "Grace, do you know who that old woman is?"

Grace turned and whispered back, "You will find out soon, Tiara. Don't worry."

Just one more secret they are keeping from me, I guess, Tiara grumbled to herself.

"Princess Tiara is called to the center," Head Servant Joseph announced.

Here it goes, she urged herself forward. With her head lowered, her eyes rapidly scanned the panorama of the room. She fisted and then un-fisted her sweaty palms, her head spinning with every step as she began to pass each brother and sister.

"Perspective," whispered Prince B.K. as Tiara walked by. The word alone caused her to pause and breathe deeply. She straightened, lifted her head, and walked on with greater assurance. Once standing before the thrones, she held her powder blue gown in hand and curtsied.

"Young Tiara," the king said directly. "What have you learned from your brothers and sisters this week?"

Glancing back at her siblings, Tiara did her best to recount the experiences of the past six days. She was purposeful to include descriptions of each virtue represented by the gems her siblings wore in their crowns.

Queen Margaret stepped forward, "Of all the virtues, which one do you believe is the most important?"

Tiara took a step back to think, for she remembered what B.K. taught her about seeing the bigger picture. She forced herself to stand still and focus.

"Well," she began, nervously curtsying again, "I do not believe I can rank these virtues in order of importance. They are all critical." Tiara went on to share what she discovered as B.K. analyzed her response to the children hurting the dog. "It was amazing to me that every single one of my brothers' and sisters' virtues were mentioned as Prince B.K. recounted my actions in the park."

King Jonathan responded, "Intriguing. It would appear that in handling the challenging situation with those cruel children, you actually demonstrated the same virtues of the other princesses and princes."

Tiara nodded thoughtfully, "Yes, I guess. I must have really learned a great deal from them!"

"Ahem," B.K. cleared his throat. All heads abruptly turned to look, surprised. "Tiara, think back on every word I said to you yesterday. There is a seventh virtue I mentioned. Did you ever figure out what it was?"

Tiara hit her forehead absent-mindedly. "Oh goodness...Oops...I mean... Oh dear, I never figured out that seventh virtue," she said nervously, nearly losing composure. "Now, let me think." She tried to remember but could not. Tiara grew anxious, and tears welled in her eyes.

As if on cue, the old woman stood up. "It was bravery," she said in a commanding voice from the side of the room. Again, everyone's focus shifted. The Old One hobbled down the aisle, carrying a large box and a huge parchment book. Desiree and Lauren quickly ran to help steady the woman, for she was without her cane. Joshua bowed and took the large box while Brittani did the same with the parchment book. Grace and B.K. moved to either side of Tiara as the guardian approached.

"Prince Burton said you were very brave," the guardian said again once she reached Tiara. "And that is YOUR virtue, young princess. You are crowned with the *virtue of courage* and your jewel will be the opal."

A collective sigh filled the Great Hall, and smiles appeared on every face. Princess Tiara dropped her jaw. She couldn't take her eyes off the woman, nor could she refrain from wiggling her knees. Grace stood close behind, placing her hand on Tiara's back once or twice. As emotions settled, the Old One took the box from Joshua. She bowed slightly before the princess and lifted out the most beautiful crown. The other children gasped in unison.

"Princess Tiara, your crown is different from the crowns worn by your brothers and sisters. Can you see there are seven jewels along the front of your crown?" Her wrinkled and bent finger pointed to each gem as she continued, beginning with the right side of the row of gems. "First there is the purple amethyst for the *virtue of righteousness*, the pink rhodochrosite for *the virtue of knowledge* is next, followed by the blue sapphire for the *virtue of humility*." Her hand moved to the other side of the crown. "See the red garnet for the *virtue of compassion*, then the green emerald for the *virtue of loyalty*, and the gold topaz for the *virtue of perspective*. Here in the center is the seventh gem, the opal, which represents the *virtue of courage*. I want you to look very closely at the opal. Tell me what colors you see."

Tiara stepped back again to study the jewel. "Why, this opal sparkles with many colors," she announced. "I thought it was a pure white, yet now I believe it reflects the colors of all other jewels in the crown. It is beautiful."

Suddenly distracted by a glowing light, Tiara gasped. "Oh my! Your cape also reflects these same colors!"

At that moment Tiara realized the brilliant flashes of color she had seen in various places of the kingdom must have come from the old woman's cape! This guardian had been with her all along. The Old One smiled, gazing intently into Tiara's eyes.

"Wear this crown with honor, Princess Tiara," she said. "For in living out the virtuous life, you must have the courage to demonstrate all the other virtues carried in the crowns of your brothers and sisters. Like the opal reflects all colors, so you must be brave enough to live your life reflecting their remarkable virtues, for that is what courage does." With surprisingly sturdy hands, the guardian lifted the crown. Tiara knelt before her as she placed it on her head.

The Old One then took the large parchment book from Princess Brittani. "This is the *Book of Truth*. Its pages contain thousands of blessed sayings for the Kingdom of Fruitful. Your parents read this sacred text together every day. The book includes all the blessings given to your siblings. It is now time to bestow your blessing. Please stand up, child."

The princess struggled to keep from fainting as she rose in anticipation of hearing her blessing. Shaking her head in unbelief, Tiara fought to keep her mouth from dropping open. This truly was a momentous occasion. The Old One turned the pages slowly until she came to the right one. Digging in the pocket of her cape, she set her reading spectacles sturdily on her nose. Then she read the blessing, *"Be strong and courageous. Do not be afraid; do not be discouraged, for the Lord your God will be with you wherever you go"* (Joshua 1:9, NIV).

Tears filled the room while the guardian closed the *Book of Truth*, placing it on the alabaster stand nearby. Suddenly, a radiance of color brighter than seen before enveloped the Great Hall. Again, Tiara searched for the source of brilliance because this time, the colors were *not* coming from the woman's cape. Instead, the lights glimmered above her. She turned around, unable to discern where the radiance came from. Prince B.K. stepped forward, bowing low enough to catch Tiara's attention. He pointed at her crown. Tiara took the crown off and could not believe her eyes. The bright, emanating glow came from her new crown.

Princess Tiara swooned with dizziness. This was all so amazing, so glorious. How could she have doubted the honor of wearing a crown? How could she have disregarded the importance of living virtuously? Gently grasping the guardian's wrinkled hands, she whispered, "Thank you, uh... by what name should I call you?"

"You may call me Old One, dear princess, for I am a simple servant sent to be your guardian. You will see me again. A guardian continually keeps watch over her charges." Brushing her wrinkled hand across Tiara's cheek, the Old One bowed. Prince Joshua stood ready with her cane, which she gratefully took to steady herself as she exited the Great Hall with surprising speed.

All in the room stood reverently still for the next few minutes. After a proper amount of time, Tiara could not restrain herself from raising her head a bit to see if her crown still radiated. It didn't matter that it had lost its exceptional brightness, for the glow in her heart was every bit as spectacular. Princess Tiara had found her virtue and would be known as *the courageous princess*.

CHAPTER 12

CELEBRATION

Head Servant Joseph and Kitchen Steward Aurora moved hurriedly to set out the special crystal dishes. The roast pork had simmered all afternoon and would be complemented by potatoes, cabbage, and carrots. Aurora baked all day to include an assortment of breads as well as Princess Tiara's favorite apple pie for dessert. Joseph offered an amused smile when she told him she'd set aside scraps of pork for Burton and carrots for Oscar.

"I'm certain Princess Tiara will be quite pleased about that," Head Servant Joseph chuckled.

Promptly at 7:00 p.m., King Jonathan and Queen Margaret arrived in formal attire, the king wearing his navy surcoat and the queen her sage green dining gown. Their diadems adorned their heads, of course. This crowning celebration would be the final one for their seven children. The king held his wife's hand high in royal fanfare as they entered the formal dining room. Kitchen Steward Aurora bowed, then hurried off to prepare the serving plates.

"Joseph," Queen Margaret instructed, "Will you be sure Princess Tiara is the last to enter the room this evening? It seems she is attached at the hip to Princess Grace these days, and we'd like to reinforce more formal protocol for this special occasion."

"Of course, your highness," Head Servant Joseph nodded as he opened wine for the king to approve.

The three older children now stood at the doorway, pleased to see their parents' happiness. Princess Desiree carried a bouquet of yellow roses which she waved lightly to get her father's attention.

"Come in, children," the king invited. Desiree and Brittani walked briskly to their mother, both kissing her on the cheek. Smoothing his surcoat, Joshua bowed slightly to his father, who promptly brought him in for a hug. "We are more formal this evening, but it doesn't mean we have to be too proper," the king laughed.

Prince B.K. and Princess Lauren followed their

siblings, both moving unpretentiously to stand behind their chairs at the round oak table. Queen Margaret caressed Lauren's back, kissing her on the cheek. Prince Joshua ambled over to his brother's side of the table and gave him a quick side shove, causing B.K. to chuckle and roll his eyes.

"We're here," Princess Grace announced, her hand threaded through Tiara's. Head Servant Joseph bent to whisper in her ear, and Grace promptly released her hold on Tiara. Grace quietly entered the room, her broad smile not to be ignored. He then whispered something to Tiara who was puzzled as to why Grace abandoned her so abruptly.

Once everyone stood behind their chairs, Head Servant Joseph nodded. Princess Tiara entered the room with slight hesitation. Her trepidation melted when she noted the warm expressions from each family member.

"I suppose I am the guest of honor tonight?" Tiara surmised somewhat nervously.

Laughter and smiles acknowledged the young princess's conjecture as Desiree promptly handed her the roses.

Tiara sniffed the bouquet's rich aroma and basked in the celebratory atmosphere. As Head Servant Joseph poured drinks, she studied the faces surrounding her. The king and queen exuded such grace, dignity, and strength. This was always true. However tonight, she also observed joy, their smiles broader than ever.

Desiree and Brittani remarked to each other about the overflowing serving plates Kitchen Steward Aurora placed on the table. Lauren and Grace asked Joshua about his upcoming polo game. He shrugged his shoulders nonchalantly, as Lauren leaned forward with widened eyes, and Grace swung her head back with a giggle.

Tiara's gaze wandered to B.K. She startled to realize he was looking directly at her. She smiled and curtsied slightly, to which he gave a quick nod.

"A toast to Princess Tiara," the king announced, lifting his goblet. "We honor you, young lady. We knew all along you possessed so many delightful attributes. You have and will continue to bless our family and our kingdom by your strength of virtue."

A subtle glow of color slowly spread across the room. Of course, all heads turned to see where the Old One was, but no one spotted her.

"That's strange," Grace offered, lifting her head up from checking under the table. "Why can't we see her?" Eyes kept searching, and heads turned one direction and then the other, but Princess Tiara stood still, smiling calmly.

"Oh, she's here," Tiara assured them as she took a step back and glanced upward. "She's here."

The End

A Sneak Peak into the Sequel

Princess Tiara and the Battle for Fruitful

Before she could finish dressing for the day, Princess Tiara heard horses' hooves outside the castle window. The thundering sound alerted her they were galloping. She rushed to the window, gasping when she saw three guards approaching the castle gates. One carried a tall black flag. She had never seen this before, but something told her it meant trouble.

Tiara dressed quickly and ran outside her bed chambers, forgetting her crown. "Brothers and sisters, wake up!" she yelled as she ran down the hall to the royal staircase. At the top of the stairs, she met Princess Desiree.

"Desiree, what is going on?" Tiara cried. "Guards on horses are approaching the castle grounds. One is carrying a black flag. We must get Father."

Though responding with poise, Princess Desiree's eyes communicated worry. "The guards are here to warn us of danger. The black flag means an enemy has been spotted, and we must get ready to defend our kingdom."

"But the Kingdom of Fruitful doesn't have any enemies. Father and Mother have always told us this."

"We certainly do not know of any enemies, Tiara. Perhaps we have one we're unaware of." Desiree hesitated briefly, then gave Tiara specific instructions.

"Little sister, you must be very brave, right now. I need you to wake up all our brothers and sisters, telling them to meet in the Great Hall right away. I am going to find Father and Mother to determine exactly what is happening. Oh, and Tiara, put on your crown. You are a princess, and you must wear your crown with dignity no matter what may happen, okay?"

Though deathly afraid, the virtue of courage she was crowned with just weeks ago welled up inside of her. Princess Tiara responded to Desiree's instructions with confidence. "I will assemble the others."

After knocking on the last bed chamber door, she glanced down the royal staircase just in time to see Coachman Klaus rushing into the castle. His shifty eyes scanned the vestibule. Tiara was relieved he didn't look up to see her observing his behavior. With shaky hands he smoothed his tunic and adjusted his cap. Then, as if performing on stage, he suddenly plastered a smile on his face, and with confident stride made his way toward The Great Hall.

What is he up to? Tiara wondered, twirling around to find Desiree. But Desiree was already out of sight. Tiara started to run down the stairs but stopped short. Nervously biting her fingernails, she worried, *what do I do? Should I follow that sneak, Klaus?* Almost immediately, she considered the opal gem in her crown, which represented courage. She paused, breathed in deeply, and decided to go straight to the Great Hall as instructed. *I will keep a very close eye on Klaus throughout the discussion. Studying his actions will give me proper perspective.*

If you enjoyed Princess Tiara's journey, please consider leaving a review on your social media pages, Amazon, and other retailer sites. Reviews and recommendations are a tremendous support to authors.

Scan or Click to Leave a Review

Additionally, asking local public and school libraries to carry the book will help provide a wholesome story about virtue for youth. My sincerest thanks.

SPECIAL OFFER!
PRINCE B.K. AND THE MYSTERIOUS PEAKS

Get a glimpse into another meaningful conversation between Princess Tiara and Prince B.K. The short story is only available to readers of *Princess Tiara and the Crown of Virtues* and provides an exclusive peak into the sequel, *Princess Tiara and the Battle for Fruitful*! **To receive your free copy, click the link or scan the QR code below.**

Princess Tiara Special Offer

A Teacher's Guide for Reading Group Discussions

Tiara and the Crown of Virtues is designed to facilitate close-reading skills as well as vocabulary development for middle grade students. The text can also be easily used as mentor text for young writers, with potential lessons as follows: using dialogue and speaker tags, incorporating metaphor, developing sentence fluency, organization and paragraphing, and word choice considerations. Below are general guidelines for questioning strategies during reading instruction. To download specific lessons (for a minimal price) on vocabulary development and writing instruction, please visit my Gumroad site at: https://jfichter. gumroad.com/

Reading Strategies to Explore

Predicting ~ After reading each chapter, students can predict what might happen in the next or future chapters. To avoid guessing, students should provide evidence for their predictions. For example, students might use this sentence frame:

In chapter _____ I read _____.
Therefore, I predict a future chapter might include details regarding _____.

Example: In Chapter Three, I read that Tiara was afraid of being late for dinner. Therefore, I predict a future chapter might include details regarding Tiara being late.

Connecting ~ Despite being a princess, Tiara is a typical twelve-year-old. Therefore, students can connect with her emotions and interactions throughout the story. A sample sentence frame for making connections might be:

I can relate to _____ in the story because I felt the same way when_____.

Example: I can relate to Prince Joshua because I felt the same way when everyone wanted to watch me play baseball this summer.

Inferencing ~ Students should be able to make inferences about the story by paying attention to the details. For example, students can imagine the internal dialogue one of the characters might have. Teachers engage students in discussions about what the story "hints" at by asking them to substantiate their reasoning with evidence from the text.

I imagine Tiara was _____.
I think this because the text describes _____

_____.

Example: I imagine Tiara was frustrated. I think this because the text describes her physically facing Desiree and crying because she was upset with the secrets she felt were being kept from her.

Synthesizing ~ Students synthesize new information with what they've already read. This allows them to revisit and possibly adjust previous inferences and predictions. A few sentence frames that help facilitate synthesizing include:

Now I understand why _____

_____.

I'm beginning to think _____

_____.

At first, I thought _____ *but now I believe*

_____.

I'm changing my mind about _____ *because now I understand* _____.

I understand this _____ *better because* _____.

Visualizing ~ Using sensory details and narrative descriptions from the story, students draw what they envision. Teachers might have them share and explain their illustrations, encouraging discussion of sensory details. Challenge students to identify similes/metaphors, or even suggest where an analogy might enhance the story.

Example: I drew a picture of Princess Grace and Princess Tiara sitting across from each other on the railings of the bridge on Singing Creek. I loved how the author described Grace placing her bouquet of flowers inside her crown. The flowers symbolize simple beauty and the sweetness of the friendship between the two sisters.

Evaluating ~ Using specific references, students can discuss what they enjoy about the story or make suggestions for improvement. Sentence frames to support this include:

*I like/dislike this event in the story*_____
*because*_____.
*A suggestion I would make to the author is*_____

_____.
When the author included _____ *, it*
helped me understand _____.
I wish the author would have included more details
about _____.

Determining Importance ~ Students identify and discuss the most important themes and messages in the story. Teachers should encourage students to justify their reasoning using evidence from the text. Sentence frames to support this include:

One important idea from the story (or this chapter) is

_____.
I think this because _____.
This detail in the story _____
is not as important. I think this because _____

_____.

The author wants us to understand _____
_____ . *I think this because the*
text includes _____
_____ .
The message of this story is _____
_____ . *The details the author uses*
to support this message include: _____
_____ .

Summarizing ~ Once students complete the story, they can identify and sequence important events that relate to the story's theme. Summarizing is different than retelling, so teachers will want to guide students to synthesize smaller details into a broader generalization of events. Students might practice summarizing at the end of each chapter, so when the story is finished, they will be familiar with the skill. A strategy for summarizing is available on my Gumroad site. https://jfichter.gumroad.com/

Acknowledgments

I wish to thank and acknowledge those who helped guide the publication of this story so dear to my heart.

- To those who ensured no component was missed: Bryan Canter (author and consultant with MyWord Publishing), Elizabeth Garrett (editor, coach, and author, Polish Point Editing), and Natasha S. Brown (cover and map design).

- To the wonderful Beta Readers who gave very helpful feedback: Stacey Stevens, Cindy Thompson, Cathy Horvath, Tiara Hooper, Allie Slocum, Vallory Darting, Lucy Floyd, Sue Janssen, Debi Curtis, Zoe Sockriter and Carol Hooper.

- To precious friends and loved ones who always cheer me on, even when they don't understand why I am constantly writing: Elmar Fichter, Kathy Robinson, Mark Hooper, Margaret Wahl, Toni Bower, Cheryl Velk, Stacey Stevens, Sue Janssen, and members of Writers on the Rock.

ABOUT THE AUTHOR

Janet Fichter writes to inspire readers to take a balcony view of challenging circumstances to gain a broader, more spiritual perspective. Having a long career in public education, she has now written a book classroom teachers can use for instructional purposes or just for simple enjoyment. *Princess Tiara and the Crown of Virtues* is a story that appeals to upper elementary and middle grade readers.

Janet is also the author of *The Ministry of the Unveiled Face* (available wherever books are sold). Her blog https://atjesusfeet.com contains both non-fiction and poetry pieces. Additionally, her writing has appeared in literary journals and anthologies.

Connect with Janet and Her Ministry

Website: www.atjesusfeet.com

Email: maggiedalene@aol.com

 facebook.com/JanetFichterAuthor

twitter.com/JFichterAuthor

instagram.com/janetfichter